Goodbye Malory Towers

Malory Towers

Enid Blyton

St Clare's
1   The Twins at St Clare's
2   The O'Sullivan Twins
3   Summer Term at St Clare's
4   The Second Form at St Clare's
5   The Third Form at St Clare's (written by Pamela Cox)
6   Kitty at St Clare's (written by Pamela Cox)
7   Claudine at St Clare's
8   Fifth Formers of St Clare's
9   The Sixth Form at St Clare's (written by Pamela Cox)

Malory Towers
1   First Term at Malory Towers
2   Second Form at Malory Towers
3   Third Year at Malory Towers
4   Upper Fourth at Malory Towers
5   In the Fifth at Malory Towers
6   Last Term at Malory Towers
7   New Term at Malory Towers (written by Pamela Cox)
8   Summer Term at Malory Towers (written by Pamela Cox)
9   Winter Term at Malory Towers (written by Pamela Cox)
10 Fun and Games at Malory Towers (written by Pamela Cox)
11 Secrets at Malory Towers (written by Pamela Cox)
12 Goodbye Malory Towers (written by Pamela Cox)

Enid Blyton

Goodbye Malory Towers

Written by Pamela Cox

Based on characters and stories created by Enid Blyton

EGMONT

Malory Towers

Enid Blyton

EGMONT
We bring stories to life

Goodbye Malory Towers first published in Great Britain 2009
This edition published 2015
by Egmont UK Limited
The Yellow Building, 1 Nicholas Road, London W11 4AN

ENID BLYTON ® Copyright © 2015 Hodder & Stoughton Ltd
Illustrations copyright © Hodder & Stoughton Ltd

Set ISBN 978 0 6035 7164 0
Book ISBN 978 1 4052 7281 0

Written by Pamela Cox

www.egmont.co.uk

A CIP catalogue record for this title is available from the British Library

Typeset by Avon DataSet Ltd, Bidford on Avon, Warwickshire
Printed in Great Britain by the CPI Group

60287/1

FSC
www.fsc.org
MIX
Paper from
responsible sources
FSC® C018306

Egmont is passionate about helping to preserve the world's remaining ancient forests.
We only use paper from legal and sustainable forest sources.

This book is made from paper certified by the Forest Stewardship Council® (FSC®),
an organisation dedicated to promoting responsible management of forest resources.
For more information on the FSC, please visit www.fsc.org. To learn more about
Egmont's sustainable paper policy, please visit www.egmont.co.uk/ethical

Contents

1	Last term at Malory Towers	1
2	The new mistress	13
3	Settling in	22
4	Good news for Edith	35
5	Gwen's missing letter	49
6	Amy's admirer	59
7	Lizzie makes a friend	72
8	Daisy is very sly	85
9	A bad time for Gwen	96
10	A super half-term	108
11	Violet plays a trick	119
12	Midnight feast	131
13	A most dramatic night	143
14	Miss Lacey's strange behaviour	154
15	Miss Nicholson saves the day	165
16	Unexpected arrivals	176
17	Reunion at Malory Towers	187
18	A shock for Gwen	197
19	A very successful gala	209
20	Goodbye Malory Towers	220

Last term at Malory Towers

'Well, Felicity,' said Darrell Rivers to her younger sister. 'Your last term at Malory Towers. How do you feel?'

'My feelings are rather mixed, to be honest,' said Felicity, taking a sip of her tea. 'I feel excited about going to university, of course. But, at the same time, I shall be awfully sad to leave old Malory Towers. I have had so many good times there, and I shall miss my friends terribly.'

'Not all of them,' said Darrell. 'Susan will be going to university with you, won't she?'

'Of course! I couldn't possibly be separated from Susan,' said Felicity. 'June and Freddie are hoping to come to the same university as us too, and so is Pam.'

'That's good,' said Darrell. 'I remember how glad I was to have a few friends around me when I started university. It must be awfully daunting to go alone.'

'I wonder if Bonnie will want to carry on her education?' said Felicity thoughtfully. 'She did awfully well in Higher Cert, you know. And the only reason she decided to take the exams in the first place was to prove a point to June.'

'She's a funny girl,' said Darrell. 'Judging from what

you've told me over the years, there's a lot more to her than meets the eye.'

'There certainly is,' said Felicity, remembering some of Bonnie's exploits. 'I thought her terribly spoilt and tiresome at first, but actually she's a very strong character, and has grown stronger during her time at Malory Towers.'

'That's one of the marvellous things about going to a good school,' said Darrell. 'If you have a good character, and are willing to learn, it will bring out all your strengths and help you to conquer any weaknesses.'

'Very true,' said Felicity, buttering a slice of toast. 'I can't think of anyone who hasn't benefited from being at Malory Towers. Even June has changed an awful lot over the last few years, and has become much more steady and responsible since she was made games captain. And as for Jo Jones – or Alice, as she calls herself now – why, you wouldn't think she was the same person.'

'I was quite astonished when you told me that Jo had returned to Malory Towers, under a different name,' said Darrell. 'I remember her so well from her time in the second form – my word, what a little beast she was then. But if she has changed as much as you say, Felicity, I shall look forward to meeting her again.'

'Darrell!' cried Felicity. 'Does this mean that you are going to come with Mother and Daddy to see me at half-term? Oh, do say you will!'

'Who knows?' said Darrell teasingly. 'I might find time to visit, or I might not. You will just have to wait and see.'

'Of course, I suppose you will have to see if you can

get time off from this new job of yours, won't you?' said Felicity. 'Won't I boast about it to the others when I get back to school – my sister an ace reporter!'

'A very junior reporter!' laughed Darrell. 'I daresay I shall be running errands and making the tea to start with.'

'Not for long,' said Felicity confidently. 'You always did have a talent for writing, Darrell. Remember that super pantomime you wrote when you were in the fifth form?'

'Cinderella,' said Darrell with rather a wistful smile. 'Yes, I still have a copy of the script. What a happy time that was!'

Darrell seemed to grow rather quiet and thoughtful then and, at last, Felicity asked, 'Is anything wrong, Darrell?'

'Oh, I was just thinking about what you said earlier,' replied her sister. 'About not knowing anyone who hasn't benefited from being at Malory Towers. You see, I can think of someone.'

'Who?' asked Felicity, surprised and curious.

'Gwendoline Lacey,' answered Darrell. 'She was in my form all the way through the school. Remember her, Felicity?'

'Oh, yes, I remember Gwen, all right!' said Felicity. 'Of course, I didn't know her nearly as well as you did, but she seemed awfully spoilt and stuck-up. Sly, too.'

'Yes, that just about sums up Gwendoline,' said Darrell rather sadly. 'She had a great many hard lessons at Malory Towers, but never seemed to learn anything from them.'

'Wasn't her father taken ill suddenly?' said Felicity.

'That's right,' said Darrell. 'At one time it looked as if he wouldn't pull through, but fortunately he recovered, though he never regained his full health. Actually, I think that Gwen did learn something from that, for she was suddenly brought to realise what is truly important in life.'

'What a horrid way to learn it, though!' said Felicity with a shudder. 'Thank heavens that Mr Lacey recovered.'

'Yes, but he wasn't able to return to his job,' said Darrell. 'Which meant that Gwen and her mother had to learn to lead a much more simple life than they had been used to.'

'That must have been very difficult for them both,' said Felicity.

'Yes, but it may also have been the making of them,' said Darrell. 'I certainly hope so.'

'Do you still keep in touch with Gwen?' asked Felicity curiously.

'No,' said Darrell. 'For we weren't close friends. Well, Gwen didn't really have any close friends. We did exchange a few letters when her father was taken ill, and she left Malory Towers, but that sort of petered out after a while. I wonder what she is doing now?'

'Well, I know what you two should be doing now!' said the girls' mother, coming into the kitchen in time to hear this last remark. 'Darrell, it's almost time for you to leave for work. And Felicity, Daddy is just loading the car up, then it will be time for us to set off for Malory Towers.'

'Heavens, is that the time?' said Felicity, glancing at the clock on the wall, before getting up from the breakfast table.

Darrell remained at the table, a rather wistful expression on her face, and Felicity asked, 'What are you thinking?'

'I was just remembering my last term,' she said with a sigh. 'I wanted to savour every moment and make it last as long as possible, and store up every memory so that I could think of my time at school fondly. And that's just what I did. I really made the most of that last term, Felicity. All of us did – except poor Gwen, of course. We worked hard and played hard.'

'That's exactly what I'm going to do,' vowed Felicity, feeling a surge of excitement, as always, at the thought of being back at school. Her last term was going to be one to remember!

The journey back to Malory Towers was very long indeed, but, to Felicity, it seemed to pass more quickly than any of the previous ones.

When the family stopped for a picnic lunch, she said as much to her parents, and Mrs Rivers said, 'It is probably because it is the last time that you will be making this journey. I expect your last term will simply fly by as well.'

'No, for I shan't let it,' said Felicity firmly. 'I am going to do as Darrell said, and make the most of every single minute – every single second!'

As the car drew closer to Malory Towers, Felicity sat up straight and gazed out of the window, drinking in every familiar landmark. There was the first glimpse of the sea in the distance, clear and blue, with the sun reflecting off its surface. And now she could see the cliffs, along which she had enjoyed so many happy walks. Then, as the car rounded a bend in the road, Felicity could see Malory Towers itself, grand and imposing, with its four towers – South, East, West and North Tower, the best one of all, for it was the one that she belonged to. And now she was going back there for the last time. As usual, on the first day of term, there was a great deal of hustle and bustle, the grounds full of people, as girls said hallo to their friends and goodbye to their parents. A big coach had just pulled up in the drive and girls poured out, most of them first and second formers.

'Oh, there's little Daffy,' said Mrs Rivers, as a small, dark girl sprang down from the steps of the coach and began chattering nineteen to the dozen with her friend. 'Doesn't she look sweet?'

'Yes, she looks sweet, all right,' murmured Felicity drily, for she knew that Daffy's looks were deceptive and hid a very naughty streak indeed. The girl had got into so much trouble in her first term that she had come very close to being sent away from Malory Towers in disgrace. The shock had been so great that Daffy had mended her ways a little, and become a lot more thoughtful and considerate. But she still had a mischievous nature, and enjoyed playing tricks, especially on poor old Mam'zelle Dupont, one of the school's two French mistresses.

As Felicity and her parents got out of the car, Daffy raced across the lawn to greet a group of her friends, all of them making a great deal of noise.

Felicity had spotted a group of her friends, too, but, as Head Girl, she couldn't sprint across to greet them as Daffy had done, much as she wanted to. Instead, she turned to her parents, saying, 'Well, dears, I shall see you both at half-term. And I shall write every week, of course.'

'See that you do,' said Mr Rivers gruffly, giving her a hug.

'Yes, for I so look forward to your letters,' said Mrs Rivers. 'Do have a good term, dear – and don't forget your night case.'

Felicity hugged her mother, picked up her night case and said goodbye, feeling glad, as she walked across to join a group of sixth formers, that her parents were sensible, and had never been the kind to indulge in long, emotional farewells.

'Felicity, you're back!'

'Nice to see you again! Had good hols?'

'Isn't it grand to be back?'

Felicity beamed round at the others – Pam, Nora, Bonnie, Amy, June, Freddie, Alice – and, of course, her best friend, Susan. How good it was to see them all again! Even the snobbish Amy looked pleased to be back.

'I say, you've had your hair cut, Amy!' said Nora, admiring the girl's sleek, golden bob. 'Very smart, I must say!'

'Are we all here?' Felicity asked. 'Oh, no, Julie and Lucy are missing. I daresay they are down at the stables.'

'And I suppose you've heard that Gillian and Delia aren't coming back?' said Susan. 'Gillian decided to take up a place at music college, and Delia is going with her so that she can have her voice trained.'

'Yes, I had a letter from Delia in the holidays and she told me,' said Felicity. 'I shall miss them both, but it's a marvellous opportunity for them.'

Gillian was a very talented musician, while her friend, Delia, had an excellent singing voice, and both girls had been very popular with the others.

'I wonder if we will have any new girls this term?' said Pam. 'Probably not, for it would be most unusual for someone to change schools in their last term.'

But, as it turned out, the girls *were* to have a new addition to their form, as they found out when they went to Matron's room to hand in their health certificates.

'Well, girls!' said Matron in her crisp tone. 'This is the very last time that I shall ask you for your health certificates. And my word, won't I be glad to see the back of you, for you've been an awfully troublesome lot!'

But Matron was smiling, and the girls knew that she was joking.

Making her eyes wide and innocent, June said, 'Matron, you surely aren't suggesting that I have been troublesome! Why, I have been as good as gold.'

'June, you are responsible for more of my grey hairs than any other girl in the school!' said Matron, shaking her head. 'And your cousin, Alicia, was just as bad in her day. I'm just thankful that you don't have a younger sister to follow in your footsteps! Now, let me have your health certificates and you can go and unpack. You are all in the same dormitory, along with Julie and Lucy, and Lizzie Mannering.'

'Lizzie Mannering?' said Nora, puzzled. 'But she's a fifth former, Matron.'

'Not any more,' said Matron. 'Miss Grayling has decided to put her up into the sixth form a term early.'

'How odd!' said Freddie as the girls made their way to the dormitory. 'I know that Lizzie is supposed to be awfully clever and studious, but it seems rather strange to separate her from her friends and put her with us.'

'Actually, I don't think that Lizzie has many friends among the fifth formers,' said Felicity. 'She was head of the form, you know, and she took it all a little too seriously for their liking.'

'That's right,' said Bonnie. 'I remember Elsie of the fifth saying that Lizzie is frightfully domineering, and doesn't care for fun and jokes.'

'Apparently she used to spend all of her spare time in the common-room studying,' said Nora. 'Imagine! And she was most disapproving of the others when they chose not to follow her lead and wanted to relax and have a little fun instead.'

'She sounds like a bit of a wet blanket,' said June, pulling a face. 'Just what we need in our last term!'

'I don't think she will try throwing her weight around with us, as she did with the fifth formers,' said Felicity. 'For we are all older than her and have been in the top form for two terms already.'

'She had better not!' said June, rather belligerently. 'Or she'll be sat on, good and hard.'

Lizzie was already in the dormitory when the others arrived and, looking at her hard, Felicity thought that she didn't look domineering at all. In fact, she looked rather scared and nervous.

Lizzie was a tall, slim girl with long, dark hair, which she wore in a thick plait over one shoulder. She had clear skin and bright blue eyes, and would have been very pretty indeed if only she didn't look so terribly serious all the time.

The girl had been arranging some things in her bedside locker, but straightened up as the others entered, looking at them rather warily.

'Hallo, Lizzie,' said Felicity in her friendly way. 'Welcome to the sixth!'

The others welcomed her too, and Lizzie said, 'Thank you. I feel awfully honoured to be here.'

'Why *are* you here?' asked June rather bluntly. 'I mean to say, what made Miss Grayling take you out of the fifth form a term early?'

'She said that, as my work was so far in advance of the others, she thought that it would do me good to go up into the sixth,' said Lizzie. 'I must say, I'm very pleased that she did, for you all seem so much more mature and sensible than the fifth formers.'

'Appearances can be deceptive,' murmured June to Freddie. Aloud, she said smoothly, 'What a shame that the fifth formers didn't live up to your high standards. I hope that we don't let you down, Lizzie.'

Lizzie was unsure how to take this, and looked a little puzzled, so Felicity stepped in, saying, 'Let's unpack quickly, girls, before the bell goes for tea. I don't know about you, but I'm starving!'

Since everyone was very hungry, they obeyed at once, and when Lizzie went to the bathroom to wash her hands, June gave a grimace. 'Lizzie might have given up her domineering ways, but she's awfully prim and proper,' she said. 'I don't like her.'

'Oh, June, do give her a chance!' said Pam. 'Why, you've only known the girl for two minutes.'

'That's long enough,' said June. 'She's the sort of person who makes me want to act all childish, and do stupid things like sticking my tongue out at her, or pulling faces.'

The others laughed, but Alice said rather hesitantly, 'I do think that Pam is right, though, and we should give Lizzie a chance. After all, you were decent enough to give me one.'

This made the others think, for Alice had first joined

Malory Towers in the second form, as the unpopular and unpleasant Josephine Jones, and had ended up being sent away. Two terms ago, she had persuaded Miss Grayling to let her join the school again, and had proved beyond doubt to the others that she had changed her ways for good.

Felicity looked at Alice, who appeared quite different now that she no longer wore glasses. Her confidence had grown too, and she was no longer the nervous, timid girl who had first joined the sixth form. Well, thought Felicity, perhaps Lizzie could change too, and realise that it was possible to take life a little too seriously at times, and there was no harm in having a little fun now and again.

The new mistress

Felicity was most surprised when, as she finished breakfast the following morning, Miss Potts, the stern head of North Tower, came over and told her that Miss Grayling would like to see her. Wondering what the Head wanted, Felicity went along to her room at once, and tapped on the door.

'Come in,' came Miss Grayling's clear voice, and Felicity entered, relieved to see that the Head was smiling.

'Well, Felicity,' said the Head, after inviting her to sit down. 'It is the beginning of your final term at Malory Towers, and I am very pleased indeed with the way that most of you sixth formers have turned out. You are, on the whole, good, kind, responsible young women, who have got the most out of your time at Malory Towers and learned all that it can teach you.'

Felicity knew very well that the Head did not just mean the lessons that could be learned in the classroom, and she flushed with pleasure.

'But there are always new things to learn,' Miss Grayling went on. 'That is why this term I have arranged some special classes for the sixth form, which I hope that you will enjoy, and which I think will be of benefit to you as you prepare to go out into the world.'

Of course, Felicity was very excited and curious indeed. What could the Head be talking about?

'A new teacher will be starting at Malory Towers this term,' said Miss Grayling. 'And she will be teaching you sixth formers such things as deportment, etiquette and so on.'

'The kind of things we would learn at a finishing school, Miss Grayling?' said Felicity, sounding most surprised, for she certainly hadn't expected this.

'That is right,' said the Head. 'I realise that some members of your form may not take to the idea as readily as others, but I would like them to attend the classes anyway, for it is always good to be open to new ideas and different ways of doing things.'

'Of course, Miss Grayling,' said Felicity rather faintly, for she wasn't too sure whether she was keen on the idea of these new classes herself!

'There is one other thing that you should know,' said Miss Grayling. 'The name of your teacher is Miss Lacey. Miss Gwendoline Lacey.'

For a moment Felicity thought that she hadn't heard the Head correctly, then she gave a little gasp.

'Gwendoline! How odd. You see, Miss Grayling, Darrell and I were talking about her only yesterday, and wondering what had become of her.'

'Well, now your curiosity has been satisfied,' said the Head with a smile. 'I realise that Gwendoline – or Miss Lacey, as you must call her now – was not the most popular of girls when she was a pupil here, but I trust that you and the others will put that behind you and treat her with the same respect you would show any other mistress. She is certainly very well-qualified to teach you in matters of etiquette and so on, for she went to a very fine finishing school herself.'

Felicity frowned at this, saying, 'I thought that Gwen – Miss Lacey – was unable to go to finishing school after her father was taken ill.'

'Fortunately her uncle stepped in and paid for Miss Lacey to take a course,' said the Head. 'Though she had to go to a school in England, and not one abroad, as she had hoped.'

'I see,' said Felicity, wondering how the others would take this news. Some of them – notably June and the tomboyish Julie – would be less than thrilled, she felt, both at the idea of having to attend the classes, and at being taught by Gwen, of all people!

But it seemed that Miss Grayling had finished with the subject, for she had now begun talking about Lizzie Mannering.

'I daresay that you were surprised to find that I had put Lizzie up into the sixth form,' said the Head.

'Yes, we were, to be honest,' said Felicity. 'I know that she is a very clever girl, but . . .'

Her voice tailed off, for she could hardly tell Miss Grayling that she thought her idea had been a strange one!

But the Head seemed to realise her dilemma, for she

smiled, and said, 'Normally I would not consider such a thing at this late stage in a pupil's education, but I considered it would be good for Lizzie, and good for the others in the fifth form.'

Miss Grayling paused for a moment, considering her words, then she went on, 'Lizzie has many good qualities, but she was not popular with the others in the fifth form because of her strictness and very serious nature. Succeeding at her studies means everything to Lizzie, and it is stopping her from growing into a well-rounded person. Also, I feel that she lacks tolerance and understanding at times. Because of this, she has not been entirely successful as head of the form, which is a shame, because I feel that she has the makings of a very worthwhile person. Perhaps she could even be a future Head Girl of Malory Towers, but only if she learns those things that she needs to learn. That, Felicity, is why I have put her into the sixth form.'

'You think that we may be able to teach her these things, Miss Grayling?' said Felicity, looking most surprised.

'I hope so,' said the Head. 'It would have been more difficult for her to learn them in the fifth form, where the girls have already formed an unfavourable opinion of her. But among new people, who are a little older and wiser than she is, and whose opinion she might value more than that of the fifth formers, I feel that she might do better. Then, when the rest of the fifth form join her next term, they will have had a break from her, and, hopefully, they will see changes in her.'

'Well, we will certainly do our best, Miss Grayling,' said Felicity.

'I know that I can rely on you,' said the Head. 'It might help if you, or one of the others, can encourage Lizzie to open up to you a little. You see, Felicity, I know a little about her home life, and I know that things haven't been easy for her. Of course, it would be quite wrong of me to say any more, but if Lizzie chooses to tell you herself, that is quite a different matter.'

Felicity was deep in thought as she made her way to the class-room, for Miss Grayling's words had brought to mind a little incident that had occurred earlier that morning.

The sixth form had been making their way to the dining-room, when they were overtaken by three giggling first formers – Daffy Hope, her friend Katie and a new girl. Daffy whispered something to the new girl that made her squeal with laughter, and Felicity, walking next to Lizzie, felt the girl stiffen beside her. Then Lizzie called out sharply, 'Edith, come here at once!'

The little first former turned, her face a picture of dismay as she walked over to Lizzie, and the sixth formers watched in astonishment as Lizzie took the girl aside and began to scold her roundly. None of them could hear what she was saying, but it was obvious from Lizzie's expression, and her tone, that she was very angry indeed, and when the first former went off to join her new friends, it was with a very subdued air.

'I say, you were a bit hard on that new kid, weren't you, Lizzie?' said Lucy. 'All the poor thing did was laugh!'

'Lizzie doesn't much care for the sound of laughter,' said June with a touch of malice. 'Do you, Lizzie?'

'That's enough, June,' said Felicity, seeing Lizzie turn red. 'All the same, Lizzie, Lucy is quite right. If you come down too hard on the youngsters over petty little things they will soon grow to resent you.'

'Yes, but you see, Edith isn't just any first former, as far as I am concerned,' said Lizzie a little stiffly. 'She is my sister, and I intend to see that she doesn't waste her time here at Malory Towers playing the fool.'

'Poor Edith!' said June, raising her brows. 'She has my sympathy, for she's not going to have much of a time of it here with you watching her every move.'

Most of the others felt the same, and Susan said, 'But she didn't do anything wrong, Lizzie. All of the youngsters get a bit over-excited on the first day of term, and even the mistresses make allowances for them, so I think that we should too.'

'Besides, your sister has to learn to stand on her own two feet and make her own mistakes,' said Pam.

'And she won't thank you for it if you keep ticking her off in front of her friends,' put in Nora. 'Take my word for it.'

'I don't mean to be hard on her,' said Lizzie, looking rather hounded. 'But I promised that I would look out for her, and I don't want to see her getting into bad company. Daffy Hope . . .'

Felicity frowned at this, for her family had been friends with the Hopes for a number of years, and she said firmly, 'Daffy is a good kid at heart. She can be a bit naughty at times, and is fond of jokes and tricks, but there is no harm in her. Anyway, there is no time to discuss it any further now, or we shall be late for breakfast, and I am sure that you don't want to set a bad example to your young sister, Lizzie.'

Felicity had glanced across at the first-form table as she ate her breakfast. She could clearly see the resemblance between Edith and Lizzie now, for the first former had the same thick, dark hair and bright blue eyes as her sister. She noticed too that the girl's blazer was a little too large for her, and the collar was beginning to fray slightly, while the skirt she wore had obviously been shortened to fit her. Were they Lizzie's hand-me-downs, Felicity wondered? Lizzie hadn't started at Malory Towers until the third form, which would explain why her old uniform was too big to fit her first-form sister.

It was clear that Edith was fast becoming friends with Daffy and Katie, for the three chattered away together over breakfast. But, Felicity noticed, Edith often looked across at her sister, a wary expression on her face, and if Lizzie was watching her, she soon fell silent.

Now, Felicity wondered if Edith had something to do with the difficult home life that Miss Grayling had hinted at, and she knew that she would have to tread very carefully indeed if she was to gain Lizzie's confidence.

Felicity was so lost in thought that, coming round a corner, she almost collided with one of the school maids.

'Oops, sorry, Daisy!' said Felicity. 'I was in a world of my own just then.'

'Oh, you did give me a start, Miss Felicity,' said Daisy, putting a hand to her heart.

Felicity hoped that the maid would not keep her talking too long, for Daisy was a great chatterbox and loved nothing more than a good gossip. Today, though, she seemed to be in a rush and hurried off without saying any more.

As she went on her way, Felicity greeted Miss Potts, who was leading a group of new girls from North Tower down the corridor, and she guessed that the mistress was taking them to see Miss Grayling. Edith Mannering was among them, looking rather nervous, and Felicity gave her a smile, which she returned shyly.

For a moment, Felicity felt wistful, wishing that she was one of the new girls, just starting out at Malory Towers, instead of finishing off. Then she remembered Darrell's words, and gave herself a shake. She mustn't waste a minute on being sad, or wishing for things that couldn't be. She had a whole term to fill with good memories for the future.

'Sorry I'm late, Miss Oakes,' said Felicity to the sixth-form mistress as she slipped into the classroom. 'Miss Grayling called me to her study.'

'Yes, Susan told me,' said Miss Oakes. 'We are just making out the time-table, Felicity, if you would like to copy it down from the blackboard.'

Felicity got out a pen and sheet of paper, and set to work. The first day of term was always nice, for there were no proper lessons. Instead, books were given out, and time-tables and lists of classroom duties were drawn up.

The sixth form seemed to have quite a lot of free periods, and Felicity guessed that some of them would be taken up by the Finishing School classes that Miss Grayling had discussed with her. Heavens, she couldn't wait to see how the others took the news when she told them at break-time.

As the sixth form were busily making out their time-tables, a taxi pulled up outside the main entrance of the school, and a young woman got out. She was well-dressed, though in rather a fussy way, a floaty scarf trailing from her neck and a huge brooch adorning her dress. As for the big, flower-trimmed hat she wore, it was really more suited to a garden party than a girls' school.

This seemed to occur to the young woman, for she hesitated outside the door and removed it, a rather apprehensive look in her eyes as she smoothed down her fluffy golden hair and picked up her suitcase.

Miss Gwendoline Mary Lacey had returned to Malory Towers.

Settling in

It was a gloriously sunny morning, and, at break-time, the sixth formers went outside and sat on the lawn, where Felicity broke the news to them about the Finishing School classes. As she had expected, reactions were mixed.

'Oh, how super!'

'What a waste of time! Who needs to learn stuff like that?'

'I think it will be jolly good fun!'

'Well, I don't. I can think of a dozen things I would rather be doing.'

'I find it quite laughable that we are supposed to learn anything from Gwendoline, of all people!' said June scornfully.

Felicity looked sharply at June, and said pointedly, 'Miss Grayling expects us to treat *Miss Lacey* with the respect that she deserves.'

'And that is exactly how I shall treat her,' retorted June. 'With the respect that she *deserves*.'

'I don't understand,' said Amy with a frown. 'Who is this Gwendoline Lacey?'

'Oh, of course, she was before your time,' said Susan.

'A few of you others won't have had the pleasure of meeting her, either.'

'Gwen was in the same form as my cousin, Alicia, and Felicity's sister, Darrell,' said June. 'And she is a sly, spiteful snob.'

'She *was*,' Felicity corrected her, with a stern look. 'She may have changed completely now, for she did go through a terrible time when her father was ill.'

'Perhaps,' said June, not sounding very convinced. 'But it sounds like she still got her way and went to finishing school, as she had always wanted. Surely, if she had been so concerned about her father, she would have stayed at home and helped her mother to care for him.'

'I quite liked the idea of Finishing School classes,' said Nora. 'Until I learned that Gwendoline was going to be taking them. I remember her making me learn a poem once, when she was in the fifth form, because she thought I had been pulling faces at her.'

'Nora, you *had* been pulling faces at her,' laughed Susan, much amused.

'Well, yes,' said Nora. 'But she could have made allowances for my youthful high spirits!'

'Gwen never made allowances for anything, once she took a dislike to someone,' said June. 'She punished me several times for the most trivial misdemeanours, but the truth of the matter was that she was using me to get back at Alicia. The two of them never got on, you know. Alicia was always making digs at Gwen, but Gwen was too afraid of my cousin's sharp tongue to retaliate.'

'I remember Gwendoline,' said Alice. 'But she may have changed, you know. It is possible for unlikeable characters to become likeable.'

'Well, you've certainly proved that,' said June, clapping the girl on the shoulder. 'But, as far as Gwen is concerned, I will believe it when I see it.'

'She sounds awful,' said Freddie, who hadn't known Gwendoline. 'But, at the same time, I'm dying to meet her just to satisfy my curiosity.'

'Yes, it will be interesting to see how she has turned out, and if she *has* changed at all,' said Pam. 'I wonder when she will arrive?'

None of the girls realised that Gwendoline was already at Malory Towers, for she had gone straight to Miss Grayling's study, where she had had a long talk with the Head.

'Well, Gwendoline,' Miss Grayling had said. 'I am pleased to welcome you back to Malory Towers as a member of staff.'

'Thank you, Miss Grayling,' Gwendoline had answered politely. 'I am very pleased to be here, and very grateful for the opportunity you have given me.'

Miss Grayling had looked at her hard, thinking that, outwardly, Gwen had not changed a great deal since her days as a pupil at the school. She was a little slimmer, and the long, golden hair, of which she had been so proud, had been cut into a more grown-up style, but apart from that she looked like the same old Gwendoline.

Had she changed inwardly, though, wondered the Head. That was what really mattered.

As their talk continued, it became apparent that Gwendoline still had the same airs and graces that everyone had disliked in her so much as a pupil. But the shrewd and wise Miss Grayling saw through them, and realised that, beneath them, was a worried and nervous young woman, striving to make her own way in the world. If only Gwendoline would stop putting on an act, how much easier she would find it! Perhaps, in time, she would come to realise that the girls would respond to her better if she dropped all her posing and behaved in a more natural way, as the other mistresses did. Gwendoline had come to Malory Towers to teach, but how marvellous it would be if she learned something as well.

Miss Grayling rang a bell on her desk and, a few moments later, Daisy, the maid, appeared.

'Daisy, please show Miss Lacey to her bedroom, so that she can unpack,' said the Head.

'Yes, Ma'am,' said Daisy, politely, before stooping to pick up Gwen's night case. 'Come this way, please, Miss Lacey.'

'Well, Daisy, so you are still working at Malory Towers,' said Gwen as she followed the maid up the stairs. 'You must have been here for quite a few years, for I was in the fifth form when you first started.'

'That's right, Miss Lacey,' said Daisy. 'I was the same age as you were then, when I began work.'

But Daisy must have led a very different life from

hers, thought Gwen, considering it for the first time. There had been no boarding school or finishing school for her, instead she had had to work, to help her family. Just as she, Gwen, was doing now. Looking at the girl, dressed in her neat, plain black dress and white apron, which all the maids wore, Gwen suddenly realised that she should be grateful for the good education she had received, for it meant that she did not have to undertake the same kind of menial work as poor Daisy. Perhaps she wasn't so badly off, after all.

Amy and Bonnie were simply thrilled at the thought of the Finishing School classes, while most of the others thought that, although they sounded like rather a waste of time, they might be good fun. Four girls, however, were very much against them. One, of course, was June. Quite apart from her dislike of Gwendoline, as games captain of the whole school she was very busy indeed and would much rather have spent the time coaching the youngsters at tennis, or arranging matches with other schools. Julie and Lucy, both of whom were rather tomboyish, couldn't see that the classes would be of any use to them at all. As Julie said, 'Why do I need to learn to walk like a fashion model when I shall be spending most of my time on horseback?'

The fourth was Lizzie, who was quite horrified that she would have to give up precious time that could have been devoted to studying.

'I will be going in for Higher Cert next year,' she said. 'And I was rather hoping that by coming up into the sixth this term I could get a head start.'

'Well, Lizzie, if you ask me, you spend far too much time poring over your books as it is,' said Felicity. 'It will do you good to think about something else. Besides, the rest of us have already taken Higher Cert, so this term is bound to be a slack one, as far as work is concerned.'

Lizzie was dismayed to hear this, and began to wonder if coming up into the sixth form had been such a good idea. She had liked being head-girl of the fifth, and had enjoyed the sense of importance and responsibility it had given her. Even if the others hadn't always seemed very grateful when she had tried to advise or guide them. But among the sixth formers she felt very small and insignificant indeed. The others were all older than she was, and there were several very strong characters in the form. Lizzie was bossy by nature, but the very thought of trying to take the lead over people like June, or Felicity, made her shake in her shoes, for she knew that they simply wouldn't stand for it and would put her very firmly in her place.

Still, there was one person at Malory Towers that she could offer guidance to – her young sister, Edith. Although Edith never seemed very grateful either!

Lizzie bit her lip as she thought of her encounter with the girl that morning. She hadn't meant to be hard on her sister, but Edith was young, and silly at times, and didn't fully realise how lucky she was to be at a good school like Malory Towers. It was vital that she made the most of the opportunity that she had been given and worked hard, and Lizzie intended to see that the girl didn't waste her time playing the fool with Daffy Hope and her friends. It was all very well for the other sixth formers to criticise, and say that she should leave Edith alone, but they didn't understand the situation, and didn't know what it felt like to be kept at Malory Towers by charity.

'I think that the classes are a marvellous idea,' said Amy. 'Don't you, Bonnie?'

'I certainly do,' said Bonnie. 'Miss Lacey will be able to teach us all sorts of things that will come in useful when we leave school.'

'Just what do you mean to do when you leave school, Bonnie?' asked Susan, curiously. 'Are you coming to university with us?'

'No, Amy and I have made a plan of our own,' said Bonnie. 'We are going to open our own dress shop. A very exclusive one, of course. Amy's father is going to lend us the money, I shall design the clothes, and Amy and I are going to run it together. With my skills and her connections I don't see how we can fail.'

Nor did the others, for Bonnie was very skilled indeed with her needle, and designed and made most of her own clothes. She was also very determined when she set her mind to something, and the girls felt certain that her venture with Amy would be a success.

'Well, I shall know where to come when I want a new dress,' said Nora. 'I wish that I had a talent like yours, Bonnie, but there's nothing that I'm particularly good at.

Mother wants me to go to secretarial college when I leave Malory Towers, but I haven't quite decided yet.'

'Well, I have decided what I am going to do, once I leave university,' said Pam. 'I would like to become a teacher.'

'Good for you, Pam!' said Julie, clapping her on the back. 'I'm sure you'll make a first-class one. And, who knows, you may end up teaching here at Malory Towers.'

'What about you, Julie?' asked Felicity. 'I bet you and Lucy both want jobs that have something to do with horses.'

'Well, my father breeds horses, as you know,' answered Julie. 'So Lucy and I are both going to work for him.'

'I'm so looking forward to it,' said Lucy, her eyes shining. 'Julie and I will be able to live together, and work together, and –'

'And eat, sleep and breathe horses!' said June, with a laugh. 'It will suit you both down to the ground. I'm hoping to train as a games teacher after I've been to university.'

The others stared at her, remembering the bold, bad, careless June who had first joined Malory Towers. Who would have thought then that she would one day want to become a teacher? The girl had had some grave faults in her character as a youngster, but she had overcome them, and, although she would probably always have a malicious streak, June had learned the meaning of responsibility and team spirit. If she had gone to another school, thought Felicity, one that wasn't as good as Malory Towers, she could have turned out very differently indeed.

Guessing at some of her friends' thoughts, June grinned, and said, 'I know, unbelievable, isn't it? But this last couple of years as games captain has pointed me in the right direction and shown me what it is I really want to do with my life.'

'Well, I can't think of anyone who would make a better games teacher,' said Felicity warmly. 'You've always been excellent at coaching, and bringing out the best in people. And, of course, none of your pupils will get away with playing any tricks on you, for you will be able to spot them a mile off, being such a joker yourself!'

Everyone laughed at this, and Pam said, 'Will you be following in Darrell's footsteps, Felicity?'

'No, because I don't have her talent for writing,' answered Felicity. 'I've always been better at things like Science and Biology. I would like to follow in my father's footsteps instead, and become a doctor. Not a surgeon, like he is, but a family doctor.'

The only one of her friends to whom Felicity had confided this ambition was Susan, and the others stared at her now, realising that the girl had chosen exactly the right career for herself. Felicity had always been kind and compassionate, and these qualities had grown within her over the years, and were just what a good doctor needed.

'How wonderful to have found your vocation,' said Alice.

30

'Yes, you're just the kind of doctor I would like to see if I was feeling under the weather,' said Nora. 'Always so calm and reassuring.'

'I'm hoping to enter the medical profession, too,' said Susan. 'But as a nurse. I say, Felicity, wouldn't it be marvellous if we could both do our training at the same hospital?'

'I wish I knew what I wanted to do,' said Freddie with a sigh. 'Still, I shall have a few years at university to think about it.'

'I'm undecided too,' said Alice. 'But I shan't starve, for Father will give me a job in his business while I think about it.'

Felicity was just about to ask Lizzie what she planned to do when she left school, but the girl suddenly spotted her young sister walking across the courtyard, and got to her feet, saying, 'Excuse me, I must just have a quick word with Edith.'

Edith was on her way to join Daffy and Katie, and her shoulders slumped as she heard her name called and saw Lizzie approaching.

'Come to tell me off again?' she said, a hint of defiance in her tone.

'Of course not,' said Lizzie, keeping her tone light. 'Why should I? Have you been up to mischief?'

'No,' answered Edith. 'But I hadn't been up to mischief at breakfast time either. That didn't stop you scolding me, though.'

'Oh, Edith, I didn't mean to scold,' said Lizzie, laying

a hand on her sister's arm. 'I promised Mother and Uncle Charles that I would look out for you, that's all.'

Lizzie had always looked out for her younger sister, and Edith had always looked *up* to her. But, after the incident at breakfast time, Daffy had said, 'I never let my big sister scold *me* like that! If you want to get the most out of your time at Malory Towers, Edith, you need to show Lizzie that you mean to stand on your own two feet and not allow her to boss you around all the time.'

'Daffy is quite right,' a girl called Ivy had put in. 'I have a cousin in the fifth, and she thought that she was going to queen it over me when I started here. But I soon set her straight and now she leaves me alone.'

Edith had realised that she was going to have to stand up to her sister if she was to win the respect of her fellow first formers. It wasn't going to be easy, for Lizzie had always ruled the roost at home, but Edith was determined, though her voice sounded more sulky than defiant as she said, 'You're just trying to spoil my fun.'

'You're not here to have fun,' said Lizzie sharply. 'You are here to work, and get good results. You know how important it is that we do well, for we can't let Uncle Charles down. It's thanks to his kindness and generosity that we are here, remember.'

'His charity, you mean,' said Edith, scowling at her sister. 'As if I am ever likely to forget.'

'Hush, Edith!' said Lizzie, as two girls walked by. 'Don't talk so loudly. We don't want everyone to know our business.'

'It's all right for you,' said Edith resentfully. 'Because you are the oldest, and bigger than me, you always have a new uniform each term, but I have to wear your ugly hand-me-downs. And they are so worn, and so ill-fitting that I shouldn't think it will be long before everyone guesses that we are poor.'

'Nonsense!' said Lizzie. 'Why, I am sure that lots of girls wear their big sisters' hand-me-downs.'

'Well, it's a pity that Uncle Charles's generosity didn't stretch a little further, so that I could at least have had a new blazer,' said Edith crossly.

'Edith, that's not fair!' said Lizzie. 'You know very well that Uncle Charles would have provided you with a complete new uniform, if it had occurred to him. But it didn't, and he has already been so kind, paying our fees, that Mother didn't like to ask him.'

Seeing that Edith looked as if she was about to argue, Lizzie went on quickly, 'Anyway, that is beside the point! You can work just as hard in a second-hand uniform as in a brand-new one. But not if you allow yourself to be distracted by the antics of Daffy Hope.'

'I like Daffy,' said Edith firmly. 'And Mother may have asked you to keep an eye on me, but she didn't say that you could choose my friends for me, Lizzie.'

'I can see that Daffy has had a bad effect on you already,' said Lizzie harshly. 'You would never have spoken to me like that before, for you always used to respect my opinion.'

'I still do,' said Edith in a more gentle tone, for she

was really very fond of her big sister. 'In some things. But how am I ever to learn to make my own decisions if you won't let me stand on my own two feet?'

Since Lizzie couldn't think of anything to say to this, it was as well that the bell which signalled the end of break-time rang.

But, as her sister ran towards the school, Lizzie stared after her, a bleak expression on her face. She simply couldn't allow Edith to waste the marvellous opportunity she had been given, and she was going to make jolly sure that the girl toed the line!

Good news for Edith

Felicity was the first of the sixth formers to meet Gwendoline. The girl was on her way to the library later that day, to return a book, when she spotted someone walking towards her. At first she didn't recognise Gwen, but as the young woman drew closer, Felicity suddenly realised who she was.

'Gwen!' she cried in surprise. Then she stammered, 'I beg your pardon! I mean, Miss Lacey.'

Gwen frowned, then her brow suddenly cleared and she said, with a smile, 'Why, it's Felicity Rivers! I hardly recognised you, for you were just a little second former when I left Malory Towers. Heavens, you're quite a young lady now.'

Felicity gave a laugh, and said, 'Well, perhaps I will be when I have attended some of your classes.'

'I certainly hope so,' said Gwen. 'Tell me, how is Darrell?'

'She's very well, thank you,' said Felicity. 'She has just started working as a reporter on a newspaper, you know. Goodness, she will be surprised when I tell her that you are teaching here.'

Felicity had been pleasantly surprised, for Gwen had

seemed quite friendly and natural. But now she gave a laugh which, to Felicity's ears, sounded rather false, and said, 'I expect that she will be. I have so much, so I wanted to do something to help others, and give something back to dear Malory Towers, as Miss Grayling has always urged us to do. The finishing school I went to was a first-rate one, you see, and I would like to put what I learned there to good use. Do give my regards to Darrell when you write, won't you, Felicity? Tell her that I'm sorry I didn't keep in touch, but I daresay she knows how it is – one is always so very busy!'

And with another, rather false laugh and a toss of her golden head, Gwen went on her way.

'It sounds as if she hasn't changed much,' said Nora, when Felicity told the others of the encounter at teatime.

'I don't know,' said Felicity thoughtfully. 'When I first bumped into her, she seemed very friendly and open. Then she suddenly put on this stuck-up act, just like the old Gwen.'

'More likely the friendliness was an act, knowing Gwen,' said June scornfully. 'I say, there she is now! She has just come in, with Miss Nicholson, the new Geography mistress.'

'What *is* she wearing?' asked Freddie with a giggle. 'Heavens, I've never seen so many bits and pieces! And that brooch she has on is the size of a dinner plate!'

'Gwen is getting more and more like her mother,' said Susan, smiling. 'I remember how Mrs Lacey always used to turn up at half-term, with scarves and veils flying everywhere.'

'I hope that Miss Grayling doesn't expect us to copy her style of dress,' said Amy, looking at the new teacher with disdain. 'I think that she looks rather vulgar.'

'Well, let's give her a chance,' said Felicity fair-mindedly. 'And her classes. Who knows, they might turn out to be good fun.'

The younger girls stared at Gwen unashamedly, for they had never seen a mistress quite like her before, and a flurry of whispering and giggling broke out.

Gwen was aware of it, turning a little pink, but she held her head high and appeared quite unconcerned as she and Miss Nicholson took their seats at the mistresses' table.

In fact, she felt very nervous indeed, particularly as many of the fifth and sixth formers remembered her from her time as a pupil at Malory Towers. And Gwen knew that their memories of her were not likely to do her any credit!

She had been very relieved indeed when Miss Grayling had told her that she was to share a study with Miss Nicholson, who, as well as being new, was young and very jolly. Gwen had dreaded that she might have to share with one of the mistresses who had taught her as a pupil, for she would have found that very awkward indeed!

She had already encountered several of the mistresses, including the stern Miss Potts, and they had welcomed her politely, but coolly, for all of them remembered the sly, stuck-up Gwendoline they had once taught. Only Mam'zelle Dupont had greeted her with warmth, for she had never seen through Gwen as the others had.

But, as silly as she was, Gwen knew that if she was to succeed as a teacher at Malory Towers, it was the good opinion of the girls that she had to win.

She felt heartened when Felicity caught her eye and gave her a smile, which she returned with genuine warmth. The others saw it too, and it made them think – perhaps Gwendoline really *had* changed for the better!

The late afternoon sun was pleasantly warm and, when she had finished her tea, June said, 'I'm off for a quick dip in the pool before prep. Anyone else fancy coming?'

Felicity, Susan and Freddie accepted this invitation eagerly, and the four girls hurried off to fetch their swimming costumes.

There were several younger girls in the pool by the time the sixth formers had got changed, and June's keen eye was caught by one of them in particular.

'My word, who's that?' she asked as the girl moved swiftly and gracefully through the water, effortlessly overtaking anyone in front of her.

'I don't know who she is, but she's jolly good,' said Felicity, watching in admiration. 'Fast, as well. I wouldn't be surprised if she could beat some of us sixth formers in a race.'

Then the swimmer climbed out of the pool, pulling

off her tight bathing cap, and Susan said, 'Why, it's young Edith Mannering!'

June was at the girl's side at once, saying, 'Edith! I was just watching you swim and you really are very good.'

Edith, quite overawed at being addressed by the games captain of Malory Towers, flushed with pleasure, and said, 'Thanks, June. I absolutely adore swimming.'

'Then I have some good news for you,' said June, grinning. 'For I want you to put in as much practice as possible. There is a swimming gala coming up in a couple of months, against four other schools in the area. And you, my dear Edith, are going to take part. Can you dive?'

Speechless with delight, Edith could only nod, and June said, 'Well, see that you practise that as well.'

Then she gave the girl a careless pat on the shoulder, before getting into the pool herself. Edith was surrounded at once by a group of first formers, all eager to offer their congratulations.

'Well done, Edith!' cried Daffy, clapping her on the back. 'June told me last term that she wants me to take part in the gala too, so we shall be able to practise together.'

'You must be frightfully bucked!' said Katie. 'I say, won't this be a bit of good news to give that sister of yours?'

'Yes, she'll be awfully proud of you,' said Ivy. 'After all, it's not everyone who has the honour of being chosen to swim for the school – and on your very first day, too!'

This hadn't occurred to Edith, and her face lit up now at the thought of how pleasant it would be to win back Lizzie's approval.

'I think that I shall go and tell her as soon as I have changed,' she said.

'Well, be quick,' said Katie. 'It will be time for prep soon!'

Edith changed quickly, then sped along to Lizzie's study, her cheeks flushed and eyes sparkling as she tapped on the door.

'Come in!' called out Lizzie, her expression most astonished as her young sister pushed open the door. 'Edith! What are you doing here? Has something happened?'

'Yes, the most marvellous thing!' said Edith, coming into the room. 'Lizzie, what do you think? June has chosen me to take part in the swimming gala! Isn't it wonderful?'

Eagerly, Edith waited for her sister's congratulations and words of praise. But they didn't come. Instead, Lizzie frowned and said, 'That's very nice, of course. But June will expect you to put in a lot of extra practice, and think how that will affect your studies. You will have to tell her that you can't do it.'

Edith's face fell as she stared at Lizzie in disbelief. 'You want me to turn down an honour like that?' she said. 'Lizzie, most girls would give anything to be chosen to swim for the school!'

'I daresay,' said Lizzie. 'But you aren't most girls,

Edith, and you don't have time for such things.'

For a moment Edith stared at her sister, then she burst out, 'I don't know why I expected you to be pleased for me! You have no time for the jolly, fun things in life, and you don't seem to care much for the honour of the school, though you should, for you have been here far longer than me. Well, I *shall* take part in the gala, Lizzie, for June is in charge of games, not you!'

With that, the girl flounced out of the room, slamming the door behind her, and Lizzie sighed heavily. This was just what she had feared, that something would happen to distract Edith from her work – but she hadn't expected it to happen quite this soon! Well, if Edith refused to back down, she, Lizzie, would just have to speak to June about it, and ask her to drop the girl from the swimming team.

It wasn't a task that she relished, however, and it took Lizzie several days to work up the courage to approach June.

Before that, there came the excitement of the sixth formers' first Finishing School class.

Miss Grayling had arranged for a disused room on the ground floor of North Tower to be cleared out so that Gwen could use it for her classes, but the door had remained locked and the sixth formers were very curious to see inside. There were to be separate classes for each tower, Miss Oakes had told the girls, for Miss Lacey felt that it was very important that she was able to give each pupil enough individual attention.

The North Tower girls felt very honoured that the new class-room was in their tower, of course.

'It makes it seem as if it belongs to *us*, somehow,' as Nora said. 'Though we shall have to let the girls from the other towers borrow it sometimes.'

They were also delighted to find that they were to be the first to use the new class-room, and all of them felt very curious indeed as they poured in on Friday afternoon. Gwen was already there, and she smiled to see the looks of astonishment on their faces as they walked in. For this was no ordinary class-room. Instead of desks and hard wooden chairs, there were sofas and armchairs. Large plants in big pots were dotted around, green velvet curtains framed the windows, and, in the corner of the room, there was a big dining table, surrounded by chairs. The room had been freshly painted in a lovely pale green, and framed pictures hung on the walls. The only thing that made it look slightly like a class-room was the large blackboard on one of the walls.

Of course, everyone was thrilled at the thought of taking lessons in such pleasant surroundings, though Amy said with a sniff, 'This furniture is awfully shabby. And the curtains have been darned.'

'I expect the room has been furnished from odd bits and pieces that have been lying around for years,' said Felicity. 'It would have cost a fortune if Miss Grayling had bought everything new.'

'Well, I believe that if a thing is worth doing it's worth doing properly,' said Amy in her haughty manner.

'Second-hand furnishings and a second-rate teacher don't bode very well, if you ask me!'

Felicity looked round sharply at Gwen, for Amy hadn't troubled to lower her voice, but she was plumping up one of the cushions and didn't appear to have heard the girl's cutting remarks.

Gwen allowed the girls a few minutes to wander round and inspect everything, then she clapped her hands together, and called out, 'Sit down, please, girls.'

At once the girls sat down, some on the sofas, others in the armchairs, several of them glancing curiously at Gwen as they did so. Most of them thought that she looked very confident and poised, but Felicity saw a hint of uncertainty and anxiety in the young woman's eyes, and realised that Gwen was not quite as sure of herself as she wanted everyone to believe. Felicity wondered if she was the only one who noticed the slight tremor in the new teacher's voice, as Gwen said, 'Well, that was your first test. Some of you passed, while others didn't.'

The sixth formers looked at one another in puzzlement, and Gwen went on, 'Pam, you flopped down on that sofa like a sack of potatoes – not very elegant! And Julie, please will you sit on the seat, not astride the arm. You are not riding a horse now!'

And so Gwen went round the class, telling this girl to sit up straight, and that one not to stick her feet out. Only Nora and Bonnie came in for wholehearted praise, Gwen telling them that they had both sat down very gracefully – 'As ladies should.'

There was one girl that Gwen didn't speak to at all, her eyes merely flicking over her coldly before moving on – and that was Amy. The girl had taken her seat every bit as elegantly as Nora and Bonnie, but not a word of praise came her way. Felicity realised then that Gwen *had* overheard the girl's remarks, and been hurt by them. Amy realised it too, and knew that she had made a bad start with the new teacher, but she shrugged it off. There was nothing that Miss Lacey could teach *her*, of that she was quite certain.

On the whole, though, most of the girls found the lesson far more amusing than they had hoped, particularly when each girl had to walk round the room, a book balanced on her head.

'Keep your back straight, Susan!' called out Gwen. 'June, don't walk quite so quickly. Oh dear, Lucy, you're supposed to glide, not stomp!'

Even Nora, Bonnie and Amy, all three of whom were naturally very graceful, couldn't manage to balance the book on their head all the way round the room, but they did very much better than the others. Again, though, while Nora and Bonnie were singled out for praise, Gwen simply ignored Amy.

'Oh dear,' thought Felicity. 'Gwen really does have it in for Amy. I do hope that it's not going to lead to any trouble.'

Felicity knew that Gwen had used spiteful and underhand methods to get back at those she disliked when she had been a pupil at the school. Surely, she wouldn't resort to such tactics now that she had grown up, and was a teacher?

Felicity spoke to Amy about it in the dormitory that evening, but the girl was unrepentant. She carried on brushing her silky, golden bob and said in a bored voice, 'I don't particularly care for Miss Lacey's opinion of me.'

'You'll care all right if she reports you to the Head,' said Felicity. 'You really shouldn't have said that she was a second-rate teacher, you know.'

Amy looked a little worried at this, for she was very much in awe of Miss Grayling, and certainly didn't want to be reported to her.

'Very well,' she said. 'I shall be all sweetness and light in the next class, and make it up to Miss Lacey.'

But alas for such good intentions, Amy had another encounter with Gwendoline the very next day.

The teacher was walking along the corridor, reading a letter, and she walked round a corner, colliding with Amy, who was coming the other way. Both the letter and the handbag that she was carrying flew from Gwendoline's grasp, the bag strewing its contents all over the floor, and she gave an irritated exclamation.

The mishap had not been Amy's fault, for Gwen had not been looking where she was going but, in an effort to make amends for her behaviour yesterday, the sixth former said politely, 'Oh, I'm so sorry, Miss Lacey. Are you hurt?'

Gwen wasn't hurt at all but, as she looked at Amy, and remembered the spiteful words that the girl had uttered yesterday, bitterness rose up within her. As it was Saturday, and the girls were allowed to wear what they pleased, Amy was dressed in a very expensive, but very simple, blue dress with a neat collar. She looked fresh and charming, and Gwen, with her frills and adornments, suddenly felt silly and over-dressed beside her.

'You silly, clumsy girl!' she snapped. 'Pick my things up at once!'

Now, Amy had been about to offer to do just that, in an effort to get into Gwen's good books, but the unfairness of the teacher's words, and her harsh tone, nettled her, and she said, 'I don't see why I should, Miss Lacey, for *you* walked into me.'

'How dare you?' gasped Gwen. 'I've a good mind to report you to Miss Grayling for insolence.'

But, even as she uttered the words, Gwen knew that she would do nothing of the kind. It would not reflect well on her, she knew, if she had to report one of the girls to the Head for cheeking her, for it might look as if she was poor at discipline.

So, instead, she said stiffly, 'I shan't report you on this occasion, Amy. But I want you to write out "I must always pay attention and look where I am going" fifty times. Bring it to my study after tea.'

Amy was simply furious at this, for she had been looking forward to a nice, lazy afternoon, and instead she was going to have to spend part of it doing a punishment that she hadn't earned at all. But she knew that to argue with the teacher might well result in greater punishment, so the girl gritted her teeth and said politely, 'Yes, Miss Lacey.'

But Amy did have the satisfaction, as she walked away, of looking back over her shoulder and seeing Gwen on her hands and knees as she picked up her belongings. Her feelings were soothed even further when she walked out into the courtyard and was greeted by Violet Forsyth of the first form. The plump little Violet had a great admiration for Amy, and she approached her now, saying breathlessly, 'Oh, Amy, how pretty you look today. That dress is so lovely.'

'Why, thank you, Violet,' said Amy, preening a little. It was a pity, she reflected, that she couldn't say the same for the first former, who was wearing a frilled, flounced creation that her mother had bought her, and which didn't become her at all. Violet, who was beginning to grow out of the fussy dresses that she had once loved, also realised that the style did not suit her and, rather nervously, she said to Amy, 'I wonder if you would mind telling me where you got the dress?'

Amy, who loved nothing better than to bask in flattery and admiration, was only too happy to give Violet this information, adding kindly, 'If you don't mind me saying so, Violet, I think that this style would suit you perfectly. Perhaps you could ask your mother to buy you something similar?'

Violet was simply thrilled at the interest that Amy had taken in her, and ran off to the first-form common-room at once, to write a letter to her mother, asking for a new dress. Her parents were very wealthy, and never refused their daughter anything, and Violet knew that it would not be long before a parcel containing the coveted dress arrived for her. Perhaps she could stop curling her hair every night, too, and have it cut into a bob like Amy's. My word, that would certainly make the others sit up and take notice!

5

Gwen's missing letter

Lizzie had settled into the sixth form in her own way, finding most of the girls pleasant and easy to get along with. There were a few that she was a little wary of, though, like the snobbish Amy, who seemed very grand indeed to Lizzie, and the sharp-tongued June, whom she was secretly a little afraid of.

Which was why Lizzie felt very nervous indeed now, as she knocked on the door of June's study, before gingerly pushing open the door. As always, June's desk was littered with papers, and the girl was frowning heavily at a list that she held in her hand. She didn't look up, and Lizzie gave a cough.

'What is it?' asked June impatiently. Then she glanced up, saw Lizzie hovering uncertainly in the doorway and her brow cleared.

'Sorry,' she said. 'I didn't mean to sound unfriendly, I was just absorbed in making out this rota for swimming practice. What can I do for you, Lizzie?'

'I wondered if I might have a word with you,' said Lizzie.

'Of course,' said June, putting down the list she had been holding. 'Come in and pull up a chair.'

Lizzie did so, but before she could speak, June said, 'My goodness, that young sister of yours swims like a fish! She's causing me some dreadful problems, though.'

'Oh?' said Lizzie hopefully, thinking that if Edith was causing problems for June, the games captain might be thinking about dropping her from the gala. Her hopes were dashed, though, when June said, 'Yes, you see she is superb at diving and swimming, so I'm really not sure which to enter her for in the gala. It's a pity that she can't do both, but I don't want her splitting herself in two, so to speak, for then I shan't get the best out her. It will be far better if she just concentrates on one or the other. Though perhaps she would want to do both? Oh, sorry, Lizzie, once I start talking about the swimming gala, I can't seem to stop! Now, what was it you wanted to say?'

Lizzie looked at June for a moment, sizing her up. She was a very downright person, who always said exactly what was on her mind, and Lizzie decided that the best way to tackle her was by being just as downright herself. So, hoping that she didn't sound as nervous as she felt, Lizzie took a deep breath, and said, 'I know that this will seem strange, but I want you to drop Edith from the gala.'

June raised her eyebrows at this, and said, 'Do you, indeed? May I ask why?'

'It's very important that Edith concentrates on her schoolwork,' said Lizzie, looking June in the eye. 'The swimming gala is a distraction.'

'Most girls seem able to fit in their schoolwork and

make time for sports and other hobbies,' said June, staring hard at Lizzie. 'And it is quite right that they should, for it is important to get a proper balance between work and play. Is this Edith's decision, or yours?'

'Mine,' answered Lizzie coolly. 'You see, June, my mother is relying on me to make sure that Edith knuckles down, and I feel that dropping her from the gala would be for the best.'

'Well, I'm sorry to disappoint you,' said June, equally coolly. 'But I have no intention of doing such a thing.'

'I am Edith's older sister,' said Lizzie, her temper rising. 'And I insist –'

But she got no further, for June was on her feet, eyes blazing. 'How dare you?' she said, her tone icy, and as stern as that of any mistress. 'You might be Edith's older sister, but I am games captain, and you don't have the right to *insist* on anything. I don't allow anyone to interfere with my decisions. Edith is taking part in the gala, and that, my dear Lizzie, is that.'

'I shall go to Miss Potts!' said Lizzie, feeling very angry herself now. 'She will back me up, I am sure.'

'And I am quite sure that she won't,' said June flatly. 'Go to the Head herself, if you wish, Lizzie, but it won't do any good.'

The two girls glared at one another for a moment, then Lizzie left the room, resisting the impulse to slam the door behind her. She went straight to Miss Potts's room, where the mistress was busy marking the first form's maths prep, and tapped on the door.

Mam'zelle Dupont, who was also there, shouted out, '*Entrez!*' and the girl went in.

'Ah, Lizzie!' cried Mam'zelle as the girl entered. Then she peered closely at the girl's pale, serious face, and said kindly, 'Is anything wrong, *ma chère*?'

'Not exactly,' said Lizzie. 'Actually it was Miss Potts I wanted to speak to.'

'What is it, Lizzie?' asked Miss Potts, looking up from her work.

Quickly, Lizzie explained the matter to Miss Potts, who, as well as being in charge of North Tower, was also the first-form mistress.

Miss Potts listened, a serious expression on her face, then she said, 'Lizzie, I can't possibly interfere in any decision that June makes as games captain. Besides, your sister is not behind in her studies in any way, so there is no reason at all why she can't take part in the swimming gala.'

'This is very true,' said Mam'zelle. 'The little Edith is excellent at French. Besides, what is it they say? Ah, I have it! *All work and no play makes Jack a dull boy!*'

Miss Potts's rather stern features relaxed into a smile at this, and she said to Lizzie, 'Mam'zelle is quite right. It wouldn't hurt you to take up some kind of sport, or hobby, Lizzie, for you are growing one-sided. I really think that you should give it some thought.'

Lizzie couldn't very well argue with Miss Potts, so she agreed that she would, then left the room – only to walk smack into June!

'So, you went to Miss Potts, after all,' said June. 'What did she say? Is she going to tell me that I can't have Edith for the swimming gala?'

Lizzie didn't reply. She didn't need to, for her flushed face and downcast eyes were answer enough, and June smiled.

'Well, I did warn you,' she said, before going on her way, whistling an annoying little tune that made Lizzie clench her fists angrily.

Dispiritedly, the girl went back to her own study, sitting down at the desk and resting her chin in her hands. A cleft appeared between her brows as she wondered what to do next. She could always write to her mother, of course, or Uncle Charles. But Mother had quite enough on her plate at the moment, and if Uncle Charles got it into his head that Edith was wasting her time at Malory Towers, he might refuse to continue paying the fees.

Suddenly, Lizzie heard footsteps in the corridor outside, followed by the sound of voices.

It was Felicity and Susan – and a thought came to Lizzie. Perhaps June would listen to Felicity. After all, she was Head Girl, and the two of them had known one another for years. Getting up, she opened the door and put her head out. 'Felicity!' she called. 'Could you spare me a moment, please?'

'Of course,' said Felicity. 'Susan, I'll meet you down at the tennis court in ten minutes.'

Then she followed Lizzie into her study, saying, 'You

really shouldn't be indoors on a glorious afternoon like this, you know. Why don't you join Susan and me for a game of tennis? I'm sure that we can find someone to make up a four.'

'Thanks,' said Lizzie with rather a strained smile. 'But I don't go in for games much.'

'Well, perhaps you should,' said Felicity, looking hard at the girl. 'You need more fresh air, for you look awfully pale. I say, is something up?'

'Sort of,' said Lizzie. And, yet again, she told the tale of what had taken place between her and June.

Felicity listened attentively, then said roundly, 'Lizzie, you're an idiot. Don't you realise what a tremendous honour it is for a first former – and a new girl at that – to be chosen for the swimming team? Edith will resent you dreadfully if you try to take this opportunity away from her, and what's more I don't blame her. You really must learn to leave her alone a bit and let her find her feet.'

Lizzie felt disappointed and let down, for Felicity was well-known for her sympathetic nature. Rather stiffly, she said, 'With respect, Felicity, you don't understand what it's like to be the eldest sister.'

'No, but I know what it's like to be the youngest,' retorted Felicity swiftly. 'My sister Darrell was in the fourth form here at Malory Towers when I started. And I know that if I had come to her and told her that I was to be in the swimming gala, she would have been as pleased as punch, and would have backed me up like anything.'

Lizzie turned red, and said, 'Believe me, Felicity, I

have Edith's interests very much at heart. I just want her to do well at Malory Towers.'

'She *is* doing well,' said Felicity. 'For she has thrown herself into life here. Not just lessons, but taking part in games and making friends. She is enjoying her time at school, and that's as it should be. I would like to see *you* taking a leaf out of her book, Lizzie. Now, I must dash, for Susan will be waiting for me. Are you quite sure you won't join us?'

'Quite sure,' said Lizzie, sounding so prim and so serious that Felicity felt quite exasperated.

What on earth was wrong with the girl? she thought, as she made her way down to the tennis court. Still, Miss Grayling felt that Lizzie was worthwhile, and Felicity had never known the Head to be wrong in her summing-up of people. As she walked through the grounds, Felicity spotted Alice in the distance. As Alice had no particular friend of her own, she and Lizzie had been thrown together a good deal, pairing up whenever any activity took place for which a partner was needed. The two girls seemed to get along well together, and Felicity wondered whether Lizzie had confided in Alice at all. She resolved to ask Alice, but there was no time now, or she would be late for tennis. Heavens, there was always so much to do at Malory Towers!

While the girls made the most of the fine weather, Gwendoline was in the study that she shared with Miss Nicholson, frantically rummaging through the drawers of her desk.

'Lost something?' said Miss Nicholson.

'Yes, a letter from home,' said Gwen, frowning. 'I had it this morning, and simply can't think where I've put it!

'It will turn up,' said Miss Nicholson in her cheerful way. 'These things always do. Have you looked in your handbag?'

At the mention of her handbag, Gwen suddenly remembered bumping into Amy that morning, and of the letter and the bag flying from her hand. She *thought* that she had picked everything up, but just suppose that she had overlooked the letter? It was a very personal one, from her parents, and the thought that one of the girls could have found it, and perhaps read it, was a distressing one.

Quickly, Gwendoline made for the door, saying over her shoulder to Miss Nicholson, 'I have just thought of somewhere I might have dropped it! I'll be back shortly.'

Gwen went back to the corridor where she had bumped into Amy that morning, but the letter was nowhere to be seen, and, frowning, she retraced her steps. What if Amy had come back and picked up the letter? She was certain to be sore with Gwen for giving her lines, and might decide to get her own back by showing it to the others.

'Hallo, Gwen,' said a cheery voice. 'Hallo, *Miss Lacey*, I should say.'

Gwen looked up, startled, for she had been so lost in her thoughts that she hadn't even heard Matron approaching. She returned her greeting, and said, 'I say,

Matron, I don't suppose that anyone has handed in a letter that they have found to you?'

'No,' said Matron. 'Today I have had a purse, a hair-slide, and – of all things – a very grubby handkerchief brought to me, but no letter. Why, have you lost one?'

'Yes,' said Gwen. 'It was from my parents, and I don't like to think that someone else might have got hold of it.'

'Well, I am sure that most of the girls here are far too well-brought-up to think of reading someone else's letters,' said Matron reassuringly. 'If one of them had found it they would have given it back to you, or handed it in to me. I daresay you've put it in a safe place and forgotten where it is!'

Gwen agreed with this and went on her way, but inwardly she felt very uneasy, for she knew that she hadn't put the letter in a safe place at all.

'No luck?' said Miss Nicholson sympathetically, seeing Gwen's downcast expression when she went back to the study. 'What a shame!'

The mistress spoke sincerely, for she knew that letters from home were very important, both to the girls and to the teachers.

'Buck up!' she said. 'You'll find it in-between the pages of a book, or something – that happened to me once. Listen, why don't the two of us pop into town for a spot of tea? That should cheer you up.'

Gwen looked into Miss Nicholson's friendly, open face and felt warmed. The other mistress was a downright, no-nonsense young woman – not the kind of person that the old Gwen would have wanted as a friend at all. Now, though, she smiled, and said, 'That would be very pleasant indeed.'

And, as the two young women walked out of the gates of Malory Towers together, Gwen reflected that she had never had a real friend in all her years as a pupil at the school. Perhaps, now that she had returned as a teacher, she had finally found one.

Amy's admirer

Gwendoline's missing letter did turn up, several days later. She and Miss Nicholson went into their study, and Gwen gave a cry as she saw the letter lying on her desk.

'Someone must have put it there while we were out,' she said. 'I wonder why whoever found it didn't return it to me immediately.'

'Oh, you know how forgetful these schoolgirls can be at times,' said Miss Nicholson. 'I expect one of them picked it up and put it into her pocket, meaning to give it to you when she saw you, and then forgot all about it.'

'Probably,' said Gwen, relaxing a little.

She had asked Amy directly if she had picked up the letter when the girl had handed in her lines on Saturday afternoon.

'Of course not, Miss Lacey,' Amy had said, getting on her high horse at once. 'If I had done so I should have given it back to you straight away.'

Gwen hadn't known whether to believe the girl or not. She had certainly *sounded* sincere, but then people who were good at telling fibs usually did.

Amy, for her part, had been most annoyed at being accused – as she put it – of taking Miss Lacey's letter, and had complained bitterly to Bonnie about it later.

'Well, to be fair, Miss Lacey didn't exactly *accuse* you,' Bonnie had pointed out. 'She merely *asked*.'

'You like her, don't you?' Amy had said, sounding rather accusing herself.

But Bonnie had merely shrugged, saying, 'I neither like nor dislike her. But I do enjoy her classes, and think that I can learn a lot from them. So I intend to stay on the right side of Miss Lacey.'

Amy smiled to herself now, as she walked to her study and remembered the conversation, for Bonnie never had any trouble in staying on the right side of people, flattering them outrageously and 'turning on the charm', as Freddie called it. And it certainly seemed to work with Miss Lacey, who was fast making a favourite of Bonnie.

Amy heard herself hailed as she opened the door, and turned to find young Violet Forsyth standing there – wearing an exact replica of the dress that she had so admired on Amy the other day.

'Look, Amy,' she said, beaming. 'I wrote to Mummy and sent her a drawing of your beautiful dress, and she managed to find one exactly like it. Isn't it super?'

'It suits you much better than all those frills,' said Amy, approvingly. 'You look very nice, Violet.'

Of course, Violet was absolutely thrilled by this praise, and she said happily, 'And Mummy's going to try and find me a bracelet like the one you wear. We shall be just like twins.'

'Well, not twins precisely,' said Amy, looking at Violet's short, plump figure and her long ringlets. 'Let's say that you will look like my younger sister.'

June and Freddie came out of June's study in time to hear these remarks, and both of them grinned broadly.

'What's this, young Violet?' said Freddie. 'A new dress?'

'Yes, and it's exactly like Amy's,' said Violet.

'Very pretty,' said June, her lips twitching with amusement. 'But I should go and get changed, Violet. It's not the weekend, you know, and if Matron or Miss Potts sees you out of uniform they're likely to take a dim view.'

'Of course,' said Violet at once. 'I just wanted Amy to see it.'

As the first former walked away, June said, 'You seem to have an admirer, Amy.'

'I know that Violet looks up to me enormously,' said Amy rather loftily. 'So, of course, I am happy to help if she asks my advice on fashion and so forth.'

'The best advice you could give her would be to work harder at tennis and swimming, and lose some weight,' said Freddie, watching Violet critically as she went downstairs. 'She would look much nicer then, and feel better.'

'Perhaps Amy doesn't want Violet to lose weight,' said June slyly. 'Imitation is the sincerest form of flattery, they say, but it won't be very flattering if your little copycat starts to look better than you do, will it, Amy?'

Amy scowled at June, while searching her mind for a withering retort, for the girl was quite right. Amy found the fact that Violet admired her so much that she wanted to copy her very flattering indeed. So much so that she was positively revelling in it! At last she said scornfully to June, 'Well, I shouldn't think anyone would ever want to imitate *your* style of dress, June. Why, sometimes you look more like a boy than a girl.'

'Oh, I don't mind that,' said June cheerfully. 'I would far rather be admired for my achievements than my looks.'

And with that, she smiled sweetly at the seething Amy, tucked her arm into Freddie's and walked away.

Violet, meanwhile, couldn't resist showing off her finery to the others, and popped into the common-room on her way to get changed.

'Violet!' said her friend Faith. 'Why are you wearing that dress? You'll get into awful trouble if one of the mistresses sees you.'

'Oh, I just wanted to try it on,' said Violet airily. 'Mummy sent it to me in the post today.'

'Very nice,' said Daffy, walking slowly around the girl. 'Er, doesn't Amy of the sixth form have a dress very similar to that one?'

Violet's worship of Amy was a great source of amusement to the first formers, and they grinned at one another. Violet, however, didn't notice, and said, 'Actually, it was Amy who told me that this style of dress would suit me. She takes *such* an interest in me, and always gives good advice.'

'I don't like her,' said Katie, wrinkling her nose. 'She's awfully stuck-up, and never even says "hallo" if she sees me, just walks by with her nose in the air.'

'Really, Katie,' said Violet, with a laugh. 'You can't expect someone like Amy to take notice of a mere first former.'

'Well, *you're* a mere first former, and she takes notice of you,' said Daffy.

'Yes, but that's because we are so alike in so many ways,' said Violet, rather smugly. 'Both of us are interested in fashion, and appreciate the finer things in life.'

'You mean that you're both a couple of vain, spoilt little snobs,' said the forthright Ivy, and some of the others laughed.

Violet scowled, but there was no time to retort, for at that moment Matron put her head round the door of the common-room, and said, 'Faith, I wanted to see you about –'

Then her eyes fell on Violet, standing in the middle of the room in her blue dress, and Matron's lips pursed, her brows drawing together in a frown. 'Violet, why are you out of uniform?' she snapped.

The girl opened her mouth to explain, but Matron swept on, 'You know very well that you are only allowed to wear your own clothes at weekends. Now, go and get changed at once, and this had better not happen again, or it will mean an order mark!'

With that she put her hand on Violet's shoulder and

steered her from the room, the others grinning as they heard Matron's voice continuing to scold as she followed the girl upstairs.

'Poor old Violet!' said Faith with a laugh. 'I must say, I can't see why she thinks Amy is so marvellous. If she has to worship one of the sixth formers, why can't she pick someone *worth* worshipping – like Felicity, or June or even Bonnie?'

'Because she's too silly to realise that their good qualities are far more important than things like wealth and good looks,' said Ivy scornfully. 'Violet is quite right, she and Amy *are* alike in some ways.'

'Well, I hope that Amy becomes bored with Violet, for she's awfully bad for her,' said Daffy. 'She was starting to behave quite sensibly last term, like an ordinary, jolly schoolgirl, but now she is slipping back into her old ways.'

Daffy and Violet had been arch-enemies when they had first started at Malory Towers, two terms ago. Daffy had hated Violet's stuck-up ways and conceit, while Violet had resented Daffy's popularity.

But then Daffy had got into serious trouble, and Violet had saved her from getting expelled, and since then the two girls had got on very much better together, a mutual respect springing up between them. The two still quarrelled at times, but without any of the bitterness they had felt before. Both of them had also been brought to see the flaws in their own characters, and had been doing their utmost to put them right.

Of course, thought Daffy, neither of them would change completely. She would always have a mischievous streak in her nature, and would always love to play tricks. But she was much more thoughtful now, and no longer played the kind of tricks that could hurt people. And Violet would never be completely without vanity, or conceit, but she had certainly improved a great deal over the past few months and the others had grown to like her much more than they had at first.

What a shame it would be if her foolish admiration of Amy undid all of that.

But, as the weeks went on, Violet continued to copy Amy in any way that she could.

If Amy had a new pair of shoes, Violet would be wearing an identical pair a few days later. When Amy appeared in the dining-room wearing a blue Alice band in her hair, Violet insisted that Faith accompany her into town on Saturday so that she could buy the very same one. And when Amy began to part her hair on the side, instead of in the middle, Violet also followed suit.

'If Amy came down to breakfast barefoot and dressed in a sack you would copy her,' said Katie, scornfully, when the first formers were in their common-room one evening.

'I wonder that you don't have your hair bobbed like Amy's, as well,' said Ivy with a sniff. 'I notice that you have stopped curling it every night.'

Violet had. She had also started brushing her hair one hundred times each night, as Amy had told her to, in the hope that it would shine like the sixth former's.

She turned a little red now, and said, 'Actually, I *am* going to get my hair cut like Amy's. As soon as my people send me some more pocket money, I shall go to the hairdresser's shop in town. But they are away on holiday at the moment, so I have to wait for them to come back before they can send me any money.' The girl sighed. 'How I wish that I didn't, for I would so like to have it cut now.'

'I bet I could cut it for you,' said Edith, looking up. 'My aunt has a hairdressing shop and I have often watched her cut people's hair. I daresay I could do it just as well as she could.'

Violet looked rather doubtful, but Ivy produced a pair of scissors from her work-basket, saying, 'Come on, then. Violet, you sit on that chair over there, and Edith can set to work.'

Violet hesitated. She wasn't entirely convinced of Edith's skill, but the girl *sounded* confident. And how wonderful it would be to go down to breakfast in the morning with a sleek, shining bob, just like Amy's, and see heads turning towards her in admiration.

So Violet sat on the chair and removed the ribbon that tied her golden hair back, while Daffy hurried to the bathroom, coming back with a towel, which she arranged over Violet's shoulders like a cape.

'So that the hair doesn't go down your back and make you itch,' she explained.

Then, under the fascinated eyes of the first formers,

and with a look of great concentration on her face, Edith began snipping away at Violet's long hair.

Alas, the girl soon discovered that it wasn't as easy a task as it looked, and as Violet's golden tresses piled up on the floor, the first formers began to look at one another uneasily.

Edith had cut quite a lot off, but instead of the neat bob Violet had wanted, her hair looked uneven and ragged, one side slightly longer than the other.

Blissfully unaware, Violet said eagerly, 'What does it look like? Is it like Amy's?'

'Er . . . sort of,' said Daffy faintly. 'Edith, I really think that you had better stop cutting now.'

Edith put down the scissors and stood back to survey her handiwork, her face falling as she realised that Violet's hairdo really didn't resemble Amy's very much at all. In fact, it looked most peculiar.

'Oh, I can't wait to see it!' said Violet, pulling off the towel and jumping to her feet.

As the first formers waited with bated breath, Violet skipped happily over to the mirror that hung on the wall.

Her happy expression turned to one of horror, then she gave a piercing shriek, crying, 'My hair! Oh, Edith, what have you done?'

'I'm sorry,' said Edith, quite aghast. 'It looked all right when I was cutting it. It was only when I stood back that I realised . . .'

Her voice tailed off as Violet wailed, 'What am I

going to do? I can't possibly go round looking like this! Everyone will laugh at me.'

'You could wear a hat,' suggested Daffy.

'Don't be ridiculous,' snapped Violet. 'I can't possibly wear a hat indoors. Potty would only make me take it off, anyway. Edith, I shall never forgive you for this.'

'Violet, I truly am sorry,' said Edith again, sounding very contrite. 'Look here, if I can just snip off that little bit of hair that is sticking up at the back, it might look better.'

She picked up the scissors again and advanced on Violet, who squealed and backed away. 'Don't you dare come near me with those scissors!' she cried.

'I think that Violet is right,' said Faith, removing the scissors from Edith's hand. 'The only thing for it is to visit the hairdressing shop and have it put right. Edith, you should really pay for it, seeing as you messed up Violet's hair in the first place.'

'Well, I can't,' said Edith bluntly. 'You know that I don't get an awful lot of pocket money, and at the moment I'm completely broke.'

'Then what's to be done?' said Violet in despair. 'I shall be the laughing stock of the whole school.'

But help was at hand. Lizzie, walking down the corridor near the first-form common-room, had heard Violet's squeals and shrieks, and been most alarmed.

Now she burst into the common-room, taking in Violet's strange hairdo, her tearful expression and the crowd of girls gathered around her.

'Violet!' cried Lizzie in horror. 'What on earth have you done? Don't tell me that you have been foolish enough to cut your own hair?'

'It wasn't me,' said Violet sullenly. 'It was –'

Then she stopped, for even silly Violet knew that it simply wasn't done to sneak, and everyone was aware how hard Lizzie could be on her young sister.

But Edith stepped forward herself, a rather defiant expression on her face as she turned to Lizzie, and said, 'It was me.'

'Well, of all the idiotic tricks!' scolded Lizzie. 'I thought that you had more sense than that, Edith. I think it's jolly mean of you to ruin Violet's hair, simply for a prank.'

'It wasn't a prank!' said Edith hotly. 'I meant to cut it properly, and I really did think that I could make a good job of it, for I have watched Aunt Mary do it so many times.'

'Well, perhaps I can tidy it up,' said Lizzie, lifting a strand of Violet's golden hair. 'I have sometimes helped Aunt Mary in the shop, for extra pocket money, and she says that I am quite good at cutting hair. Sit down, Violet.'

Violet looked very nervous indeed at the thought of another of the Mannering sisters cutting her hair, but she didn't dare disobey a sixth former, and sat obediently.

'Lizzie really is very good,' said Edith reassuringly. 'She cut Mother's hair for her in the holidays.'

Certainly, Lizzie seemed a lot more skilled than her young sister as she set to work tidying up Violet's hair, snipping off a bit here, and a bit there. At last she was finished, and Lizzie clapped her on the shoulder, saying, 'All done. Go and have a look in the mirror.'

Once again, rather apprehensively, Violet went over to the mirror and looked at her reflection. What she saw there made her want to burst into tears. Lizzie had certainly done a good job, and the girl's hair looked very neat and tidy. But, because Edith had cut it so raggedly, Lizzie had had to cut it very much shorter than Violet wanted, in order to get it even.

Hardly able to get the words out for the lump in her throat, she said tonelessly, 'Thank you, Lizzie.'

'That's quite all right,' said Lizzie. Then she turned to her sister, and said sternly, 'I hope that this has been a lesson to you, Edith. If you had been occupied with something useful, such as studying, you wouldn't have had time on your hands to make such a mess of Violet's hair.'

Then she went from the room, closing the door behind her.

'Take no notice of her,' said Daffy, patting Edith on the arm. 'I know that she's your sister but, my goodness, she's awfully domineering.'

'Don't I know it!' said Edith ruefully.

Then Daffy turned to the unhappy Violet, saying, 'Cheer up! It suits you much better than those long curls. You look like a proper, sensible schoolgirl.'

'But I don't *want* to look sensible,' moaned Violet. 'I want to look –'

'We know!' chorused the others in exasperation. 'Just like Amy!'

Lizzie makes a friend

Of course, somehow the story of how Edith had ruined Violet's hair, and Lizzie had come to the rescue, soon flew round the school, and poor Violet had to endure a great deal of good-natured ribbing when she came down to breakfast the following morning.

She felt rather hurt when Amy herself teased her about it. But, seeing that the girl was upset, and not wanting to lose her faithful admirer, Amy quickly said, 'It might not look exactly like mine, but it will soon grow. I think that it would look better if you clip the front back with a hair-slide. I have a very pretty one that would be just right, so if you would like to come to my study later, I shall give it to you.'

So, thrilled at the thought of getting a present from Amy, Violet soon cheered up, and didn't even mind too much when Mam'zelle Dupont exclaimed over the loss of her beautiful golden curls.

One good result of the affair was that Lizzie went up a little in the estimation of the sixth formers, for dealing so well with the situation.

'It was jolly decent of you to step in,' said Alice to Lizzie, in the courtyard on Saturday afternoon. 'Though

I must say, I should have liked to see Violet's hair after your young sister had cut it. My word, she must have looked a fright!'

Even Lizzie couldn't suppress a grin at this, as she said, 'She did. It's just lucky that I happened to be near the kids' common-room and heard all the commotion.'

Alice glanced at Lizzie, pleased to see her smile for a change.

The other day, Felicity had spoken to Alice, and asked her how she got on with Lizzie.

'All right,' Alice had replied with a shrug. 'She is very difficult to get to know, for there is something rather stand-offish about her. She never talks about her home, or her people, and even in her spare time she would rather sit with her head in a book than do something just for fun.'

'Do me a favour, would you, Alice?' Felicity had said. 'See if you can bring Lizzie out of herself a bit, and see if you can get her to think of something other than work for a change. I really think that it would do her the world of good.'

'I shall do my best,' Alice had said, feeling rather proud that Felicity had entrusted her with the task of befriending Alice, and she had sought the girl out several times. Lizzie, who knew very well that she wasn't enormously popular, had been surprised to find that Alice wanted her company. Her responses to Alice's attempts at conversation were not very encouraging, however, for although Lizzie was always perfectly polite, she always managed to give the impression that she was in a hurry to get back to her books.

Encouraged now by Lizzie's smile, Alice said, 'It's a simply glorious day. How about coming for a walk along the cliffs?'

'That sounds nice,' said Lizzie, politely, 'but I have some reading that I must be getting on with. Miss Oakes told me that we will be studying the Tudors for Higher Cert next term, so I am getting a head start on the others who will be coming up into the sixth next term.'

'I didn't go in for Higher Cert myself,' said Alice. 'I don't have the brains for it, you see. But I did help some of the others study, and I remember copying down reams of notes on the Tudors for Felicity. I wonder if she still has them, for I am sure you would find them most useful.'

'Oh, it would be marvellous if she would lend them to me!' said Lizzie eagerly.

'Well, I shall ask her,' said Alice. 'But you must do something for me in return. Slack off a bit this afternoon and come for a walk with me.'

Lizzie bit her lip. A walk in the sunshine would be very pleasant, and if Alice really could get hold of Felicity's notes for her, they would come in very useful. So she nodded, and said, 'Very well. If I can get hold of Felicity's notes it will save me an awful lot of trouble in the long run, so I daresay that I can spare a little time.'

Felicity, watching the two girls walk towards the gates a few minutes later, was pleased. What an achievement for Alice, to get Lizzie away from her books for a while!

Most of the sixth formers were outside, making the most of the good weather. Julie and Lucy had gone horse-riding, June and Freddie were down at the pool, coaching the first and second formers, while the others lazed on the grass.

Only Amy and Bonnie were indoors. Bonnie was in her study, engrossed in a tablecloth that she was embroidering for her mother, and humming softly to some music on the radio as she worked. Amy, meanwhile, was making her way to Miss Lacey's class-room, a large bunch of sweetly scented flowers in her arms.

Miss Lacey had been showing the girls how to arrange flowers in vases, making use of ferns and foliage to create an artistic effect, and it had been decided that, each week, the girls would take turns to do a flower arrangement for her class-room.

It had been Bonnie's turn last week and, as the girl had a flair for such things, her arrangement had been very pretty, and Miss Lacey had been pleased with it. This week, though, it was Amy's turn, and the teacher had condemned her effort as very poor indeed.

'It doesn't look as if you have even attempted to create anything pleasing to the eye, Amy,' Miss Lacey had said with a sniff. 'You have simply stuck the flowers into the nearest available vase, without any thought of arranging them prettily.'

In fact, this was exactly what Amy *had* done, for she found flower-arranging a dreadful bore and simply couldn't see the point of it!

'When you are married, and have your own home, you will want it to look nice, won't you?' Miss Lacey had said.

'Of course,' Amy had replied, in her haughty way. 'But I shall have a housekeeper to see to such dull chores as arranging flowers.'

Miss Lacey had looked simply furious, two spots of red darkening her cheeks, as she glared at Amy, but before she could vent her anger on the girl, Bonnie said in her soft voice, 'Oh, Amy, flower-arranging isn't a chore! Why, it's an art, isn't that so, Miss Lacey?'

Bonnie's words, her soft voice and the way she looked admiringly at Miss Lacey, soothed the teacher a little.

'I am glad that there is someone in the form who realises that,' she said, giving Bonnie a warm look. Then her voice hardened as she turned back to Amy, and snapped, 'This won't do at all. Amy, I must insist that you pick fresh flowers and make a new arrangement tomorrow.'

Amy had scowled, and as Miss Lacey moved away Bonnie hissed under her breath, 'Idiot! Why do you persist in getting on the wrong side of Miss Lacey? You know that she will only end up punishing you.'

'I don't care,' said Amy with a shrug. 'At least I don't suck up to her like you do.'

'You can think yourself jolly lucky that I stepped in just then,' said Bonnie severely. 'If I hadn't, I think you might have got a worse punishment than just having to do the flowers again!'

Amy was forced to admit that this was true. She also knew that she was only hurting herself by antagonising Miss Lacey, but somehow she couldn't seem to stop herself, for her dislike of the young teacher grew more intense with every day. But the feeling was entirely mutual, for Miss Lacey didn't like Amy, either, and showed it very plainly.

Now, as Amy went towards Miss Lacey's class-room, she saw Violet Forsyth approaching, and smiled at the girl.

'Hallo, Amy,' said Violet. 'My word, what lovely flowers.'

'Yes, it is my turn to do the flowers for this week,' said Amy. 'But my efforts at arranging them didn't meet with Miss Lacey's approval, so I have to do them all over again. It's utterly pointless doing them on a Saturday, for by the time the class-room is used again they will be all wilted. It's just spite on Miss Lacey's part, so that I have to give up part of my weekend.'

'What a shame that I can't help you,' said Violet. 'I sometimes help Mummy to do our flowers at home, and I have quite a knack, you know.'

Amy looked down into Violet's eager face, and a thought occurred to her. Miss Lacey's classroom was strictly out of bounds to all but the sixth formers, and it was kept locked when there were no classes taking place. Amy had got the key from Daisy, the maid, so that she could do the flowers. But it had suddenly occurred to the girl that she could finish her task much more quickly with Violet's help.

So she leaned forward, and said in a conspiratorial whisper, 'Violet, how would you like to see inside Miss Lacey's class-room?'

Violet, of course, was simply thrilled, for she – like the rest of the first form – was very curious indeed to see inside the locked room. How marvellous to be able to boast to the others that she had actually been inside!

This hope was dashed, though, when Amy held up a warning finger, and said, 'You mustn't let anyone know that I have taken you in there, or I would be in the most awful trouble! It must be our secret.'

Violet was disappointed that she wouldn't be able to tell the first formers of her adventure but, in a way, it would be just as nice to have a secret from them, something that only she and Amy knew about.

So the girl promised solemnly that she would not tell anyone at all, and Amy gave her the flowers to hold while she quickly unlocked the door. Then – after glancing swiftly up and down the corridor, to make sure that no one was about – she ushered Violet inside, closing the door.

Violet had never seen a class-room like this one before, with its armchairs and sofas, and the elegant velvet curtains hanging at the windows.

'How marvellous!' she breathed, gazing around her.

Amy, extremely gratified at the younger girl's reaction, quite forgot that she had criticised the furnishings as being shabby and said airily, 'Much nicer than an ordinary class-room, isn't it?'

'I should say!' breathed Violet. 'Amy, do you think I might try one of the sofas? They look so comfortable!'

Amy looked on indulgently as Violet tried the sofas and the armchairs, pronouncing that they were very comfortable indeed, and so much more elegant than the hard chairs in the first-form class-room. Then Amy glanced at her watch, and said, 'I suppose we had better get on and arrange these flowers. Violet, be a dear and fetch a vase from that cupboard, would you?'

Violet did as she was asked, then Amy sighed, and said, 'Oh dear, how difficult it is to know where to start! I really have no talent for this sort of thing at all.'

'Let's start by putting the taller flowers in the vase,' said Violet, picking one up. 'Then we can arrange the smaller ones around them.'

The first former proved to be surprisingly nimble-fingered, and Amy soon found that she had nothing to do but stand back and watch, which – of course – suited her perfectly.

Violet, meanwhile, was in her element, for not only was she doing something which she genuinely enjoyed, but she was spending time with Amy, revelling in the honeyed words of praise that fell from the sixth former's lips.

'That ought to please Miss Lacey,' said Amy as Violet put the finishing touches to her arrangement. 'How disappointed she will be not to have an excuse to scold me!'

'You know, Amy, I wouldn't be a bit surprised if Miss

Lacey wasn't jealous of you,' said Violet. 'She always tries hard to look fashionable and elegant, yet somehow she never manages to look as nice as you do. In fact . . .' Violet gave a little giggle. 'The way that Miss Lacey dresses rather reminds me of my mother.'

Amy laughed at this, pleased with both the compliment, and the dig at Gwendoline.

But before she could reply, the door suddenly opened and Daisy stood there. 'I came to see if you had finished, Miss Amy,' she said. 'So that I can take the key back to the housekeeper.'

Then she spotted Violet, and said, 'Miss Violet, you know that you shouldn't be in here! This room is for the sixth formers only.'

'Oh, Daisy, do be a sport and don't sneak on us!' said Amy, giving the maid a pleading look. 'Violet wasn't doing any harm, really she wasn't.'

'I really should report this to Miss Potts,' said Daisy, looking stern. Then, looking at the two rather scared faces before her, she relented and said, 'I'll let you off this time – mind, it's only because I'm scared of that Miss Potts, and I don't like talking to her if I don't have to. Now be off with you, Miss Violet, and don't let me catch you in here again!'

Relieved, Violet scuttled away, while Amy said to Daisy, 'Thanks awfully. You're a good sport, Daisy.'

'That's as may be,' said the maid with a sniff. 'But you're old enough to know better than to break the rules, Miss Amy. What Miss Lacey would say if she knew about all this, I don't know.'

The snobbish Amy didn't at all care to be scolded by a maid, but it wouldn't do to upset Daisy, so she said meekly, 'You are quite right. I shan't let Violet in here again.'

Daisy seemed satisfied with this, and she and Amy left the room, Amy locking the door behind her and handing the key to the maid. Then the two of them went their separate ways, Daisy to return the key to the housekeeper, and Amy to go in search of Bonnie.

Lizzie, meanwhile, was finding her walk with Alice unexpectedly enjoyable.

'Do you know,' she said to Alice, 'I have been at Malory Towers for two whole years, and yet I have never walked along the cliffs before!'

'Well, now that you know how enjoyable it is, I hope that you will make the time to do it more often,' said Alice.

The two of them had found a sunny spot overlooking the sea and were sitting on the grass.

'My word, only two weeks until half-term,' said Alice. 'I can't believe how the time has flown. Will your parents be coming, Lizzie?'

'There is only Mother,' said Lizzie. 'For Father died when Edith was small, you know. I doubt very much that she will be able to come, because she had to take a job when Father died and she works so terribly hard all the time.'

Alice was very sorry to hear this, but she was also rather curious, as she knew that the fees at Malory Towers were expensive, and it sounded as if Lizzie's mother was not terribly well-off. So how on earth did she manage to keep two girls at Malory Towers?

Almost as though she had guessed what Alice was thinking, Lizzie said, 'Our Uncle Charles pays our school fees, Edith's and mine. He is Father's older brother, and we are very grateful to him.'

'I should think you must be,' said Alice. 'It's awfully generous of him.'

Lizzie gave a tight little smile, but said nothing, and rather an uncomfortable silence fell.

Alice broke it by saying, 'Shall we make our way back to school now? I don't want to be late for tea, for this fresh air has given me such an appetite!'

Lizzie agreed at once, and the two girls took the cliff path back to Malory Towers, coming out near the swimming-pool.

'It looks as if June is still coaching the youngsters,' said Alice, putting a hand up to shield her eyes from the sun as she watched some of the first and second formers climb out of the pool. A lone diver stood poised on the topmost diving-board.

'I say, isn't that your young sister up there, Lizzie?' Alice asked. 'I've heard that she's absolutely marvellous at swimming and diving. Let's get a closer look.'

As they moved nearer, Edith launched herself from the diving-board, doing the most beautiful swallow dive, and entering the water with barely a splash. She really was very graceful to watch, and the spectators, who had all stood in enthralled silence as Edith dived, now burst into a round of spontaneous applause.

Edith turned red with pleasure as she climbed out of the pool, and June went across to clap the girl on the back, crying, 'Jolly well done, Edith! My word, you will certainly shine at the gala. You really are a wonder!'

Lizzie, overhearing, felt a pang. There was such pride in June's voice, and in her face. And Edith, thrilled, was hanging on the games captain's every word, looking up at her in the same worshipful way that she used to look at her older sister.

Oh, it just wasn't fair, thought Lizzie bitterly. She almost felt as if June had stolen Edith away from her, for the girl obviously looked up to her no end, while she, Lizzie, had become almost an enemy. Out of the corner of her eye, she could see Alice watching her, a curious expression on her face, and Lizzie knew that the girl was wondering why she didn't go and make a fuss of her young sister, and tell her how well she had done.

The odd thing was that as Lizzie had watched Edith glide gracefully into the water, she *had* felt proud of her – intensely proud. But she couldn't bring herself to go to the girl and tell her that, for to do so would only encourage her to waste even more time on swimming and games. And, no matter how good she was, Edith would never be able to make a career out of swimming, and earn good money at it, and that was what mattered.

Just then Edith turned, and saw Lizzie watching. She smiled at her big sister, hoping that she would come across and speak to her. But Lizzie merely waved, before turning away and saying to Alice, 'Come on, let's go and wash our hands before the bell goes for tea.'

Edith's shoulders slumped, some of the joy fading from her face, and several of the others noticed it.

'Never mind about Lizzie!' said Daffy, giving her arm a squeeze. 'I know that she is your sister, but she really is a misery!'

June had noticed too, and she stared after Lizzie and Alice as they walked away, a hard expression on her face.

If Lizzie wasn't very careful indeed, she thought, she was going to end up pushing her young sister away completely.

Daisy is very sly

There were three letters beside Gwendoline's plate when she came down to breakfast on Monday morning, and Miss Nicholson exclaimed, 'Heavens, someone's very popular! Don't tell me that it's your birthday?'

'Oh, no,' said Gwen, picking up the envelopes as she sat down. 'This one's from Mother, and this is from Miss Winter, my old governess. I recognise their writing.'

Then she frowned as she picked up the third one. 'The writing on this one looks vaguely familiar too, but I simply can't think whose it is.'

Gwen read her mother's letter without much enthusiasm as she ate her scrambled eggs. Mrs Lacey had never fully adjusted to the more simple way of life that the family had adopted since her husband's illness and, as Gwen had expected, her letter was just a list of complaints and grumbles.

Gwen sighed as she laid it aside and opened Miss Winter's, which was much more cheerful in tone. The young woman smiled fondly as she read it, for she had grown to appreciate Miss Winter far more in recent years than she had as a spoilt schoolgirl. The old governess really had been a tower of strength to the whole family, particularly to her mother, since Mr Lacey had been taken ill. Not that Mother would ever admit that, of course!

Gwendoline herself often felt ashamed when she thought of how, as a young girl, she had rather despised poor, plain Miss Winter, and taken her adoration for granted. Now, though, she understood her situation a great deal better, and felt very grateful indeed for the woman's affection and friendship.

It took Gwen a while to read Miss Winter's letter, for it was a long and chatty one, but at last she finished and slit open the third envelope. Then she gave a gasp.

'Anything wrong?' asked Miss Nicholson, looking up sharply from her plate.

'No, not at all,' said Gwen. 'It's just that this letter is from someone I haven't heard from in simply ages. One of the girls who used to be here, at Malory Towers with me, in fact.'

The letter was actually from Darrell, for Felicity had told her sister that Gwen was now teaching at the school. Gwen was surprised at how pleased she felt to hear from Darrell, for the two of them had never been close friends. But Darrell had been kind to her when her father had been taken ill, something which Gwen had never forgotten.

Her letter was packed with news, and it was obvious that Darrell was leading a full and enjoyable life, making the most of every moment, just as she had when she had been at Malory Towers. There was also news of some of the other Malory Towers girls who had been in her form

– Sally, Alicia, Irene, Belinda, Mavis and Mary-Lou, and Gwen began to feel quite nostalgic as she read it. Then, at the end of the letter, Darrell had written something that brought a wide smile to Gwendoline's face.

Oh, my goodness! thought Gwen. How marvellous! How simply splendid! I shall write back to Darrell this very evening!

Over at the sixth-form table, Felicity had also received a letter from Darrell, and she read parts of it out to the others.

'Darrell is simply thrilled that I am to be in the swimming gala,' she said. 'Oh, how super, she's promised to take me out to tea in the holidays if I do well.'

'How marvellous!' said June. 'Of course, Darrell is the kind of sister who would always back you up in whatever you chose to do.'

June flicked a glance at Lizzie as she spoke, and the girl, knowing that the words were aimed at her, flushed.

'Alicia is just the same,' went on June. 'Though, of course, she is my cousin, and not my sister. But she was terribly proud of me when I became games captain, and sent me such a nice, encouraging letter.'

Susan, not realising that June was getting a dig in at Lizzie, said, 'How nice it must be to have an older sister – or cousin, in your case, June – to look up to and share good news with. I have often wished that I had one.'

'I'm sure that you are not alone in that wish, Susan,' said June smoothly.

Lizzie scowled at June. Since she had tackled June

about dropping Edith from the swimming gala a few weeks ago, Lizzie was not in as much awe of her as she had been. But she was still a little afraid of June's sharp tongue and sharp wits, for it was rare indeed for anyone to get the better of the girl in an argument.

So Lizzie held her tongue and said nothing, though it was really very difficult, especially when she saw June go up to her sister after breakfast and lay a friendly hand on her shoulder, while Edith looked up at her admiringly. Daffy and Katie were there too, and it was plain that they both thought that June was a most wonderful person as well. As the three first formers moved away to go to their first lesson, Lizzie called out Edith's name, but her sister did not turn round.

Lizzie was quite convinced that Edith had heard her, though, and was simply pretending not to because she didn't want to talk to her. Lizzie felt hurt and angry, for although she knew that she was sometimes hard on Edith, she was very fond of her younger sister, and everything she did was for the girl's own good. What a beastly day this was turning out to be!

But someone else was having an even worse day than Lizzie. Gwen was in a good mood as she unlocked the door of her class-room that morning. The letter she had received from Darrell had cheered her up enormously, and she was pleased to see that the West Tower sixth formers had arrived early for their class and were waiting for her to unlock the door. She greeted them brightly, for they all looked keen and that boded well for the lesson.

But when Gwen unlocked the door and stepped inside, she gave a little groan, putting her hand up to her throat.

'What is it, Miss Lacey?' asked a plump, kindly girl called Christine.

'See for yourself,' said Miss Lacey in a trembling voice, standing to one side.

The West Tower girls poured inside, and a collective gasp went up. For the flowers that Violet had so carefully arranged two days ago had been taken from their vase and strewn higgledy-piggledy about the room. Some had been thrown on the chairs and sofas, others were on the floor, and still more had been thrown on to the big table. The water from the vase had been poured over Miss Lacey's desk, ruining some papers that she had left there. And the lovely glass vase, one that Gwen had brought herself from home, had been thrown against the wall and was smashed to smithereens. The West Tower girls exclaimed in horror.

'Who on earth could have been mean enough to do this?'

'Could it have been meant as a joke, do you suppose?'

'If it is a joke, it's not very funny.'

'This is no joke, it's sheer spite! Anyone can see that!'

'Well, let's set to work and clean up,' said Christine briskly, seeing that Miss Lacey was in a state of shock, and taking charge. 'Vera, Joy and Nancy, you begin picking up the flowers,' she went on. 'Jane, can you clear the papers from Miss Lacey's desk, and I will sweep up the broken glass.'

Gwen, who hadn't moved or spoken since she had seen the damage done to her lovely class-room, sank down into an armchair, looking very pale, and Christine said, 'Tessie, can you fetch Miss Lacey a glass of water, please?'

'Of course,' said Tessie, hurrying from the room.

Miss Potts, who happened to be walking down the corridor, spotted her, and called out, 'Where are you off to in such a hurry, Tessie? Shouldn't you be in Miss Lacey's lesson?'

'Yes, Miss Potts,' said Tessie. 'But something terrible has happened, and I am just going to get some water for Miss Lacey. She really does look as if she might faint, you know.'

Heavens, what on earth can have happened? thought Miss Potts, frowning, as Tessie continued on her errand. I had better go and investigate.

The mistress walked into Miss Lacey's class-room, her lips pursing as she took in the scene before her. Girls bustled about, clearing up the mess, while Miss Lacey sat huddled in an armchair, looking – as Tessie had said – as if she might faint at any moment.

The girls stopped what they were doing when Miss Potts entered, standing politely to attention, and the mistress said, 'Carry on, girls.'

Then she sat down next to Miss Lacey, and said in a low tone, 'What has happened here?'

'I don't know,' said Gwen in a tremulous tone. 'The room was like this when I unlocked the door this morning. I simply can't think who could have done this, or why.'

'The door was locked, you say?' said Miss Potts.

'Yes, it is always kept locked when it is not in use,' said Gwen. 'Only myself and the housekeeper have keys.'

'Well, I hardly think that the housekeeper would have done such a thing,' said Miss Potts, looking very puzzled indeed. 'I wonder if anyone else could have got hold of her key?'

Suddenly Gwen remembered something, and gave a gasp. 'Amy had the key on Saturday! It was her turn to do the flowers for the room, and she was going to get the key from the housekeeper.'

'Then we had better speak to Amy,' said Miss Potts, looking rather grim as she stood up. 'I shall tell her to come to my room at break-time.'

Amy was puzzled, and a little alarmed, to receive a message saying that Miss Potts wanted to see her at break-time. Oh dear, what if Daisy had broken her word and told the mistress that Violet had been in Miss Lacey's room on Saturday? Not only would she be in trouble with Miss Potts and Miss Lacey, but the rest of the form would be angry with her too.

When the bell went for break, she made her way to the study that Miss Potts shared with Mam'zelle Dupont. Mam'zelle was not there, but Miss Lacey was seated next to Miss Potts, looking very upset.

'Sit down, Amy,' said Miss Potts, sounding very stern. Then she went on to tell Amy of the damage that had been done to Miss Lacey's classroom.

'I am not accusing you of anything, Amy,' she finished. 'I am simply giving you an opportunity to own up if you do know anything.'

'Miss Potts, the room was in perfect order when I left it,' said Amy, looking the mistress straight in the eye, and sounding rather dignified. 'That is the truth. Why, I would never dream of doing such a thing.'

Miss Potts believed the girl at once. Amy could be spiteful at times, but her spite usually took the form of making cutting remarks about the others. She had never been one for playing mean tricks on people. Miss Lacey, however, was not so convinced, and she said, 'Is there anyone who can confirm that?'

Amy hesitated for a moment. Violet could confirm it, of course, but Amy couldn't possibly tell the two mistresses that she had allowed the first former into the classroom, for then both of them would be in trouble. Then she remembered that someone else had been there.

'Yes,' she said. 'Daisy, the maid, came along just as I was finishing off. We left the room together, then I locked the door and handed her the key, to give to the housekeeper. She will be able to tell you that I left the room as I found it.'

'Good,' said Miss Potts, sounding relieved. It didn't solve the mystery, but at least Amy's name would be cleared. 'I shall send someone to fetch Daisy.'

'I can go and find her, Miss Potts,' said Amy, for a thought had just occurred to her. Daisy had given her word that she would not sneak, but she had not known then that she would have to face the stern Miss Potts. It would be as well to have a quick word with the maid before she was questioned, decided Amy, to make absolutely sure that she didn't give the game away.

A third former told Amy that she had just seen Daisy making her way up to the dormitories with a pile of clean linen, and the girl quickly caught up with her.

'Daisy!' she said. 'I must speak with you at once.'

'Why, whatever is the matter, Miss Amy?' asked Daisy, startled.

'Come in here, where we shan't be overheard,' said Amy, taking the maid's arm and pulling her into the sixth-form dormitory.

Quickly she told Daisy of what had happened. The maid's eyes were big and scared as she said, 'And now Miss Potts wants to question me?'

'That's right,' said Amy. 'But all you have to do is tell her that the room was neat and tidy when I locked the door, which is perfectly true.'

'Yes,' said Daisy hesitantly. 'But what if it comes out that a first former was in there with you?'

'Daisy!' gasped Amy, shocked. 'You promised that you wouldn't tell.'

'I won't,' said Daisy. 'Well, not on purpose, anyway. The thing is, you see, that Miss Potts frightens the life out of me, with her stern voice, and her cold eyes, and that way she has of looking at you over the top of her glasses. She gets me that flustered, there's no knowing what I might say!'

Daisy had moved across to the little cabinet that stood beside Amy's bed as she spoke, and she picked up a bottle of perfume that stood there, taking out the stopper and sniffing at it. 'My, this is lovely,' she said. 'No wonder you always smell so nice, Miss Amy. How I wish that I could afford expensive perfume, but there's not much chance of that on the wages I earn.'

'Look here, Daisy,' said Amy. 'If you promise to keep your nerve when Miss Potts questions you, and not to mention Violet, I shall give you the perfume to keep.'

Daisy's eyes lit up, and she said eagerly, 'Do you mean that, Miss Amy?'

'Yes,' said Amy. 'But you must keep your part of the bargain, see, otherwise I shall take the perfume back.'

'Oh, I won't sneak, no fear of that,' said Daisy, slipping the perfume bottle into the big pocket of her starched, white apron. 'I shall run along to see Miss Potts this very minute.'

The maid almost skipped from the room, and Amy watched her go, a frown coming over her face. She regretted having to give her lovely perfume away, but that wasn't what was troubling her. It seemed to Amy that there had been rather a sly look on Daisy's face when she picked up the perfume. Had that been the maid's intention all along – to get an expensive present from Amy, in return for her silence?

A bad time for Gwen

Word of the damage that had been done to Miss Lacey's classroom soon spread around the school, and the North Tower sixth formers, in particular, felt very dismayed when they heard the news.

'I know it's silly, but I feel as if that room belongs to us more than any of the others, because it is in our tower,' said Nora.

'I wonder who can have done it?' said Pam with a frown.

'Someone with a very mean, spiteful streak, obviously,' said Susan scornfully. 'I hope that whoever it was feels thoroughly ashamed of herself.'

The girls were sitting on the grass outside, enjoying the brilliant sunshine, and Freddie, who had been lying on her back, shielding her eyes with her hand, suddenly sat up and, lowering her voice, said, 'Of course, you know that Miss Lacey suspected Amy, don't you?'

'Yes, I had heard a rumour,' said Felicity. 'But Daisy was able to clear her name, fortunately.'

'I can't say that Amy has ever been my favourite person,' said June. 'But I don't think that she would stoop to that kind of low trick.'

'Nor do I,' said Felicity. 'It's rather horrible to think that it must have been a sixth former, though.'

'What makes you say that?' said Alice, startled.

'Well, obviously someone has a grudge against Miss Lacey,' said Felicity. 'And as we are the only form that she teaches, that rather rules out the lower forms, for none of them know her well enough to have taken a dislike to her.'

'That's very true,' said Susan. 'I wonder if it could have been someone from another tower?'

'Well, I know that Jane from West Tower doesn't like Gwen,' said June, who steadfastly refused to refer to the new mistress as Miss Lacey. 'And that South Tower girl, Elspeth, dislikes her heartily.'

'And let's not forget that you aren't too keen on her either, are you, June?' said Lizzie with a little laugh. 'I don't suppose it could have been you, could it?'

It was said lightly, but everyone knew of the animosity between Lizzie and June. Felicity braced herself to intervene, as they all waited with bated breath for June's withering retort. But, to the surprise of the sixth formers, the girl merely laughed, and said, 'Actually it could easily have been me. Or you, Lizzie, or Felicity, or Susan – or any one of us.'

'Don't!' said Nora with a shudder. 'It's horrible to think that we are all under suspicion.'

'Well, we are,' said June bluntly. 'For the key to Gwen's class-room hangs on a hook in the housekeeper's room. It would have been an easy matter for anyone to slip in while she was out and take it. Why, even one of the mistresses could have done it.'

Freddie gave a laugh, and said, 'Who do you suspect, June? Mam'zelle Dupont, perhaps?'

The others laughed too, as they pictured the plump little French mistress sneaking into Gwen's class-room and wreaking havoc. Then June said, 'Probably not, for she never saw through Gwen and I believe that she is quite fond of her. But there is no denying that she wasn't popular with most of the mistresses when she was a pupil here.'

'Oh, I simply can't believe that any of the mistresses would do such a thing!' exclaimed Felicity. 'Why, most of them have been here for years!'

'Miss Nicholson hasn't,' said Alice thoughtfully.

'No, but she and Miss Lacey seem to be good friends,' said Susan.

'Yes,' said June. 'But perhaps that is Miss Nicholson's way of trying to avoid coming under suspicion.'

'I refuse to listen to any more!' cried Nora, clapping her hands over her ears. 'It's simply horrible to think that someone as downright and jolly as Miss Nicholson could play mean tricks on someone who is supposed to be her friend.'

'Of course it is!' said Felicity. 'We shall probably never find out who was responsible, so let's just hope that whoever wanted to get her own back on Miss Lacey will think that she has done enough and won't take things any further.'

But Miss Lacey began to go through a most annoying time over the following week. A photograph of her mother, which she kept on the desk in her study, was removed from its frame and torn into tiny little pieces. Then someone cut the flower off her favourite hat when she left it on a bench in the courtyard one day. And worse was to come.

Going into her bedroom one Saturday afternoon, Gwen was horrified to discover that her chest of drawers had been ransacked, the contents strewn about the bed and the floor. She gave a little cry of horror, the tears that had always come so readily when she had been a schoolgirl starting to her blue eyes. But Gwen blinked them back resolutely, gritting her teeth as she began picking up stockings and handkerchiefs, and putting them away tidily again. Someone obviously had it in for her, and was trying to make her time at Malory Towers as miserable as possible – perhaps they even meant to drive her away. But they would not succeed. Gwen could not let them succeed, for she needed this job and the money it brought in, and so did her family. Then as Gwen put her scattered things away, she made an unpleasant discovery. A pair of cufflinks that she had bought her father for his birthday, and hidden in one of the drawers, was missing. A lump rose to her throat, for she had badly wanted to buy her father something special, and had been putting a little money aside each week, picturing his surprise and delight when he opened her gift. As she fought to control her tears, a cheerful whistling came from outside, and Gwen, recognising it, pulled open her bedroom door and said, 'Miss Nicholson! Come here a moment, would you?'

Miss Nicholson entered the bedroom, frowning as she saw her friend's distressed expression.

Quickly, Gwen explained what had happened, her voice breaking slightly as she told the other mistress about the missing cufflinks.

'This is quite dreadful!' exclaimed Miss Nicholson, sounding most concerned. 'The other things that have happened to you – as horrible as they are – can be dismissed as mere spite, but this is theft. You must report it to Miss Potts, or even to Miss Grayling, at once.'

But Gwen was strangely reluctant to do this, and, when pushed by Miss Nicholson, she admitted, 'If I tell Miss Grayling about the cufflinks, all the other things will come out too.'

'Well, that's a good thing, if you ask me,' said Miss Nicholson stoutly. 'It's about time that the person who is playing these beastly tricks knew that we are taking it seriously, for it might make her think twice before playing the next one.'

'Yes, but don't you see?' said Gwen, a bleak look on her face. 'If all of this comes out, Miss Grayling might decide that it is too much trouble to keep me on here as a teacher. Oh, I know that the girls play tricks on the staff sometimes, just as they did when I was a pupil here. But it is all done in good humour, and this is quite different, for there is so much spite in it! Whoever heard of a teacher who was so unpopular that someone hates her enough to steal from her, and spoil her things?'

'Well, if you refuse to report it, we shall just have to do our utmost to thwart whoever is doing this ourselves,' said Miss Nicholson, a very determined expression on her round face. 'You must make sure that you lock your bedroom door from now on, every time you leave it.'

'That's just it, though, I thought that I *had* locked it,' said Gwen with a puzzled look. 'But I suppose I must have been in such a hurry that I forgot. I saved so hard for those cufflinks too.'

'Look here,' said Miss Nicholson gruffly, laying a hand on Gwen's shoulder. 'I can lend you the money if you want to buy another pair, and you can pay me back a little at a time.'

Gwen flushed, deeply touched by her friend's offer. But she had been brought up not to borrow or lend money, and she said, 'It's awfully kind of you, but I simply couldn't. I'm afraid that Father will have to be content with a set of handkerchiefs.'

'Just as you like,' said Miss Nicholson. 'But the offer stands if you change your mind. Now, let's put the rest of your things away and go down to tea. And this time, make sure that you lock the door behind you!'

Lizzie, meanwhile, had been pleasantly surprised when her young sister had agreed to take a stroll with her.

'I went along the cliffs with Alice the other day,' she

said. 'And the views are simply marvellous. Do let's, Edith! It seems such a long time since we spent some time together.'

Edith had looked a little doubtful, and, seeing her expression, Lizzie had laughed, and said, 'I will promise not to mention the swimming gala, or June, or your friendship with Daffy.'

'All right,' Edith had said with a grin. 'I shall hold you to that.'

And the two sisters had talked and laughed together as they strolled, making it seem quite like old times.

'How the weeks have flown,' said Lizzie, as the two stood looking out to sea. 'Next weekend it will be half-term.'

'How I wish that Mother could come,' said Edith, rather wistfully.

'So do I,' said Lizzie, squeezing her sister's arm. 'Still, it won't be so very bad. At least we will have one another, so we shan't be quite alone.'

Edith bit her lip, and cast a sidelong look at Lizzie.

'Actually,' she began, rather hesitantly. 'Actually, Lizzie, Daffy has asked me to go out with her and her people. And I – I said yes.'

'Oh!' said Lizzie blankly. She had pictured herself spending the day with Edith, trying to make up to her for their mother's absence. And now it seemed that the girl didn't need her after all!

'I'm sorry,' said Edith, hanging her head. 'I was so thrilled to be asked that it never even occurred to me that you would be alone too. Of course, I shall tell Daffy that I can't go with her.'

But Lizzie, looking down at her sister, took a sudden, noble resolve, and said, 'You'll do nothing of the sort!'

Edith looked up in surprise, and Lizzie went on, 'As if I would ask you to give up such a treat! Of course you must go with Daffy. Don't worry about me, for I will be quite all right.'

'Are you sure?' said Edith, her brow clearing. 'Oh, of course you will be all right! One of the sixth formers is sure to ask you out. In fact, I thought that you would probably have had one or two invitations already.'

'Oh, I have,' said Lizzie airily. 'I turned them down because I didn't want to leave you on your own, Edith, but now that I know you are going out with Daffy I shall be able to accept one of them. It looks as though we are both going to have a marvellous half-term.'

Lizzie spoke cheerfully, for she didn't want to dampen her sister's spirits, but actually no one had asked her to go out with them at half-term. In fact, Alice was the only one who knew that Lizzie's mother wasn't coming, and she had assumed that the girl would not want to leave Edith on her own, so had not bothered to invite her out.

Normally, the thought of an extra day to herself, to pore over her books, would have been a very welcome one, but it would be hard to think of studying when the others were all having a happy time with their families. Suddenly Lizzie began to feel very lonely, and to realise that the others had a point when they said that there was more to school life than studying. If only she hadn't cut herself off from the others quite so much, she might have more friends, and wouldn't be facing the bleak prospect of a lonely half-term.

This thought was on Lizzie's mind when she went into tea and, seeing her miserable expression, Alice said in a friendly way, 'Is something the matter, Lizzie?'

'No, nothing at all,' said Lizzie, forcing herself to smile, for she was far too proud to admit to Alice that Edith had been asked out at half-term.

'Well, you look as if you have all the cares of the world on your shoulders,' said Susan. 'For goodness' sake, cheer up! There's only a week to go until half-term.'

'Perhaps that is what's upsetting Lizzie,' said June smoothly. 'We all know how she hates to tear herself away from her books. And heaven forbid that she should actually have some fun!'

Lizzie couldn't even bring herself to retort to this, but Alice said rather sharply, 'Oh, do be quiet, June. I'm sure that Lizzie is looking forward to spending the day with her sister just as much as the rest of us will enjoy being with our families.'

Felicity threw Alice an approving look, and said, 'Oh, isn't your mother coming, Lizzie?'

'No, she can't get away,' said Lizzie, trying her hardest not to sound too mournful.

'What a shame,' said Pam. 'But it's a good thing that you will have Edith to keep you company.'

Lizzie could have told the others then that Edith was

spending half-term with Daffy, but somehow she couldn't bring herself to say it. Alice, or one of the others, might feel sorry for her, and feel obliged to invite her to go with them. And Lizzie didn't want anyone's pity. So she merely nodded, and said, 'Yes, it should be a pleasant break.'

But Alice, who knew the girl a little better than any of the others did, was puzzled. Something was definitely bothering Lizzie. And Alice found out what it was quite by accident.

She was in the changing-room after tennis practice one afternoon when Daffy and Katie came in. Neither of them saw the sixth former, for she was seated behind a row of lockers.

'I'm so excited about half-term!' said Katie. 'Father said that my older brother may be coming as well, and I can't tell you how much I'm looking forward to seeing him again.'

'Yes, it will be fun,' said Daffy. 'Edith is coming out with my people, for her mother can't come, you know.'

'I don't think that Mrs Mannering is terribly well off,' said Katie. 'For Edith told me that she can't afford the train fare to Malory Towers. Still, I'm sure that she will have a marvellous half-term with you.'

'I suppose anything is preferable to being with that miserable, domineering Lizzie,' said Daffy. 'Although I must say, she seems to have taken the news that Edith won't be able to spend half-term with her jolly well. I think that several of the sixth formers have invited her to go out with them.'

The two first formers chattered for a few more minutes as they changed, then they left, their voices fading away.

Alice, who knew very well that no one had invited Lizzie to go with them, sat deep in thought. So, Lizzie had pretended to her sister that she had plans of her own, so that Edith could go off and enjoy herself without feeling guilty. Well, that was all very fine and noble, but why on earth couldn't Lizzie just come out and admit that she felt upset about spending half-term on her own? If Alice had known that Edith was going with Daffy, she would have asked Lizzie to join her people. And, no doubt, a few others would have extended invitations too, for the sixth formers were a good-hearted lot, on the whole. Lizzie must have known that.

She *did* know it, thought Alice, suddenly realising what was preventing Lizzie from telling the others that she would be on her own. It was foolish pride, pure and simple. Alice remembered the way that Lizzie had suddenly seemed to close up when she had been talking about her uncle paying her school fees, and Edith's. The girl didn't like to think that she was at Malory Towers because of someone else's charity, and she didn't want the others to know it either. And what had Katie said? Mrs Mannering couldn't afford the train fare to the school. Yet Lizzie had told Alice that her mother couldn't come because she was too busy – her pride again. And she didn't want the others pitying her, and feeling that they had to ask her to join them, that was why she hadn't told anyone that Edith would be going out with Daffy and her people at half-term. Alice gave a sigh. It was very good to have pride, of course – pride in one's school, one's family and one's self. But the kind of pride that Lizzie had was just foolish, and was going to make her very unhappy in the long run. Alice was quite determined that Lizzie wasn't going to spend half-term alone, but she knew that she would have to approach the girl very carefully. How was she to go about it, though?

10

A super half-term

Alice wracked her brains, and at last she came up with a plan for inviting Lizzie out, without revealing that she knew Edith was spending half-term with Daffy.

Lizzie spotted Alice going into her study one evening, looking rather preoccupied, and, remembering how kind the girl had been to her, she went across and said, 'Anything wrong, Alice?'

'Oh, hallo, Lizzie,' said Alice. 'Well, nothing is wrong, precisely, it's just that . . .'

She paused, looking up and down the corridor, then went on, 'Look here, can you come into my study for a moment? I don't want to be overheard.'

'Of course,' said Lizzie, surprised and a little alarmed. Whatever could Alice have to say to her?

The two girls sat either side of the desk in the little study, then Alice leaned forward and said in a confiding manner, 'The thing is, Lizzie, I'm absolutely desperate to find someone who will come out with me and my people at half-term, and I just can't think of *anyone*! Julie's parents can't come, but she has already arranged to go with Lucy, and Nora thought that her people might be busy, but it turns out that they are going to be able to come after all. Oh dear, what am I to do?'

'But, Alice, I don't understand,' said Lizzie with a frown. 'Why is it so important that someone comes along with you at half-term?'

'So that I can convince my mother and father that I have settled down here and made friends,' explained Alice. She looked Lizzie in the eye, and said, 'It's no secret that I was once sent away from Malory Towers, when I was in the second form.'

Lizzie nodded, for although she had not been a pupil at the school in those days, she had heard the story.

'It was partly because my parents didn't back me up in the right way,' Alice continued. 'And partly because I was such a horrid little beast that no one wanted to be my friend. But now that I have turned over a new leaf, my parents have done the same, and they are keen to come along and see how I am doing. Mother wrote and said that she would be so thrilled if I could bring a friend along with me at half-term. I know that it would help convince her that I really am doing well at Malory Towers now.'

Lizzie bit her lip. She had grown to like Alice very much, and it would certainly be much more pleasant to go out with her and her people at half-term than to stay at Malory Towers alone, watching everyone else enjoying themselves.

Alice sensed that she was wavering, and said, 'It's a shame that you will be with Edith. I would really have liked you to come with me, Lizzie, for Mother said that she would like to meet my best friend. And I suppose that *you* are my best friend, for I seem to spend more time with you than with anyone else.'

This was all that Lizzie needed to hear, and, turning red with pleasure, she said, 'Well, actually, Alice, I won't be with Edith, for she has been invited out by Daffy Hope and her people.'

'Really?' said Alice, sounding most surprised. Then she sighed, and said, 'I suppose that I am too late, though. No doubt someone else has invited you to go along with them.'

'No, no one has,' said Lizzie. 'And I would simply love to come out with you and your people, Alice.'

'Would you?' said Alice, with a smile. 'Good, well, that's settled then.'

The next few days simply flew by, and the girls grew very excited indeed as half-term drew closer and closer.

The younger ones, in particular, became very boisterous, but most of the mistresses were lenient, and made allowances for their high spirits. Even Miss Potts let Daffy, Katie and Edith off with the mildest of scoldings when the three of them skipped the whole length of the corridor, almost knocking over one of the maids, who was carrying a tray of crockery to the kitchen.

At last the big day arrived, and soon cars lined the driveway, and the school became a hive of activity as girls greeted their parents and eagerly showed them around.

Felicity was delighted to see her mother and father,

of course, but she was a little disappointed that Darrell was not with them.

'I did think that she might be,' she said to June, who was standing nearby. 'For she said to me as I left that she might see me this term.'

'That's funny, Alicia said something similar to me when I saw her in the hols,' said June. 'I half expected her to turn up as well, but there's no sign of her.'

But despite Darrell's absence, Felicity enjoyed a marvellous half-term, going out for lunch on both days with her parents, taking part in the diving exhibition, and going to bed thoroughly worn out, but very happy.

All of the sixth formers were very curious to see Alice's parents, particularly her father, who they remembered very well from her time in the second form.

Alice's father had been a very loud, ill-mannered individual indeed, and although Lizzie had never met him, the others were full of stories, and she felt rather nervous.

But it seemed that Mr Jones had changed his ways, for the man who greeted Alice with a hug was polite, quietly spoken and rather subdued.

He and his wife took the two girls for a picnic on the beach on Saturday, and to a very nice restaurant on Sunday. The restaurant was a rare treat for Lizzie, whose mother had little money to spare for such luxuries, and she enjoyed herself enormously, and thanked Alice and her parents profusely when half-term was over.

The first formers, of course, had had a whale of a

time, and as several of them had birthdays coming up, some of the girls came back with money or gifts.

'My parents have given me some money so that I can have some sort of party,' said Katie.

'And mine,' said Ivy. 'And my grandmother has promised to send me a big birthday cake.'

Violet also came back with a hamper full of goodies, even though it wasn't her birthday. But, as Daffy said, Violet's parents never seemed to need an excuse to spoil her!

'Look at this!' said Violet in the common-room on Sunday evening as she pulled one thing after another from the magnificent hamper. 'Tins of prawns and pineapple, chocolate, shortbread biscuits – oh, and a gingerbread cake!'

'How super,' said Edith enviously.

'We really should have some sort of feast, you know,' said Daffy. 'It's your birthday soon, Katie, and Ivy's. We could make it a joint celebration.'

This suggestion found instant favour.

'Oh yes, do let's!'

'My word, wouldn't that be wonderful!'

'We really should. It must be at least two terms since we last had a feast.'

'When and where, though?' said Katie.

'Well, your birthday is next Saturday, Katie,' said Ivy. 'And mine is the following Monday, so why don't we have it in the middle – on Sunday?'

'Marvellous idea!' said Faith. 'I suppose we could have

it in the dorm, though it's a little cramped in there.'

'The common-room would be better,' said Edith. 'Though it's a little close to the study Mam'zelle and Miss Potts share, and I know that Mam'zelle often sits up late at night.'

'Oh, it would simply ruin things if Mam'zelle heard us,' said Daffy. 'I say, what about having it outside? I remember my sister, Sally, telling me that the upper fourth had a feast by the pool once. They went for a swim, as well.'

'How super!' said Ivy, her eyes lighting up.

'Well, it would have been,' said Daffy. 'Only it began to rain, so they had to go back indoors after all.'

'I really think it would be safer to hold it inside,' said Faith. 'I suppose it will have to be the dorm.'

'Perhaps not,' said Violet, who had been listening to all of this with a thoughtful expression. 'I know of somewhere else we might be able to go.'

'Where?' asked everyone eagerly.

Violet, however, adored being mysterious and having a secret, and refused to say any more for the time being. But she had thought of a rather daring plan, one which she was quite certain even Daffy would not have come up with, and she was certain that she would go up in the estimation of the first formers when they learned what it was.

For Violet intended to get hold of a key for Miss Lacey's class-room, and hold the feast there. It was far enough away from the studies or dormitories for any slight noise to go unheard, and they would be able to have their feast in elegant surroundings. What could be better? Of course, Amy had told Violet about all the fuss there had been when the flower arrangement had been smashed, so the girl knew that they would have to be very careful and clear away any mess after they had finished. And she also knew now that the key was kept on a hook in the housekeeper's room, so it should be quite simple to sneak in and borrow it.

So the first formers went ahead with their plans for the feast, trusting Violet to find a safe place for them to hold it. There was a large cupboard in their common-room, and Violet placed her hamper on the big bottom shelf.

'With the things Ivy and I will buy with our birthday money, there should be more than enough for everyone,' said Katie.

'Well, we others will contribute something too,' said Faith. 'It's only fair, as you two – and Violet – are being generous enough to share with us.'

Over the coming days, the cupboard filled up as the first formers stored their contributions to the feast. Edith managed to save a small amount from her meagre pocket money, and bought two tins of condensed milk. But as she was on her way to the common-room with them, who should she bump into but her sister, Lizzie.

'Hallo, Edith,' said Lizzie. 'It's not like you to be indoors on a glorious day like this.'

At once, Edith flushed guiltily, and she quickly hid

the bag containing the tins behind her back. But Lizzie's sharp eyes spotted the movement, and the guilty look, and she said, 'What are you up to, Edith?'

'N-nothing,' stammered poor Edith, doing her very best to look as innocent as possible. 'I just need to fetch something from the common-room.'

'What are you holding behind your back?' asked Lizzie sharply. 'And don't say "nothing", for I can see quite clearly that you have something there.'

'Just a little shopping,' said Edith, feeling that it was terribly bad luck that she should have run into her sister.

'Oh?' said Lizzie. 'I'm surprised that you have any money to go shopping, Edith, for I know exactly how much pocket money you have, don't forget.'

'Well, I managed to keep a little back, so that I could buy some things that I needed,' said Edith. 'Some shoelaces and a new hair ribbon.'

'Let me see,' said Lizzie, growing more suspicious by the second. Edith's manner was so very odd.

'No!' said Edith defiantly. 'What I choose to spend my pocket money on is none of your business, Lizzie.'

She stepped forward, determined to put an end to the conversation, but as she did so, the paper bag containing her purchases slid from her grasp, and the two tins of milk rolled across the floor.

Swiftly, Lizzie stooped and gathered them up, her mind working quickly, then she glanced at her sister, who had turned very red indeed, and said, 'These are the funniest looking shoelaces I have ever seen. You first formers are planning a midnight feast, aren't you?'

Edith knew that there was no point in denying it, for her face gave her away. If Lizzie had been different, she could have told her all about it, and although her big sister might have pretended to look stern and wagged her finger, there would have been a twinkle in her eye, and they could have laughed about it together. But there was no twinkle in Lizzie's eye, and Edith began to feel angry, as she said, 'What if we are? It has nothing to do with you.'

'Well, that's just where you're wrong,' said Lizzie in a harsh tone. 'I am a sixth former, and it is my duty to see that the rules of the school are kept.'

Edith gave a gasp, and cried, 'But what harm are we doing? It's only a feast.'

'Which means that you will be tired the following day, and unable to concentrate on your lessons,' said Lizzie severely. 'You can't possibly expect to work well if you are up half the night.'

'Do you mean to say that you would get the whole of the first form into trouble just to make me knuckle down?' asked Edith, looking her sister in the eye.

Lizzie hesitated. *Was* she prepared to go that far? The truth was that she simply didn't know, but she wasn't prepared to make an empty threat. So she said heavily, 'I shall have to think about this, Edith. I will let you know what I decide.'

And with that, Lizzie turned on her heel and walked away, leaving her sister staring after her in dismay.

Of course, Edith had to tell the others, for she had to warn them that there was a chance Lizzie might sneak on them, so a meeting was called in the first-form common-room that evening.

'Blow!' said Ivy when Edith broke the news. 'If it had been any other sixth former, I daresay they would have been decent about it and turned a blind eye. Not Lizzie, though, mean beast.'

Edith flushed, for it was not pleasant to hear her sister spoken about in this manner.

'Lizzie *might* not tell,' she said.

'Might isn't really good enough,' said Daffy crossly. 'We need to be absolutely certain that Lizzie won't sneak on us.'

'Edith, please tell me that you weren't silly enough to tell your sister *when* we are holding the feast,' said Katie.

'Of course I wasn't!' said Edith hotly. Then, in a more subdued tone, she added, 'Not that it matters. Lizzie will be watching us like a hawk now.'

'Oh well,' said Ivy with a sigh. 'I suppose that settles it. The feast is off.'

'It doesn't have to be cancelled altogether,' said Faith. 'We can hold a party at teatime, instead.'

But this idea found no favour with the first formers at all.

'Where's the fun in that?'

'It just won't be the same!'

'Sneaking out of our beds at midnight is what makes the party special.'

'No, the midnight feast *will* go ahead!' said a very determined voice, and everyone was surprised to see that it was Edith who had spoken. She got to her feet now, and said, 'I will see to it myself that Lizzie doesn't interfere. Even if it means missing the feast so that I can keep an eye on her.'

The first formers, who had all felt a little cross with Edith, immediately thawed towards her, and Faith said, 'Well, that's awfully decent of you. I must say, it would have been terribly tame if we had had to hold the party at teatime, instead of at midnight.'

'Well, you won't,' said Edith firmly. 'I shall make sure of that.'

11

Violet plays a trick

Two days before the first formers' feast, Miss Nicholson walked into the study that she shared with Miss Lacey, looking very pale and heavy-eyed.

'My goodness, you look dreadful!' exclaimed Gwendoline. 'Whatever is the matter?'

'Toothache,' groaned poor Miss Nicholson, putting a hand to her jaw. 'I've scarcely slept a wink.'

'Well, you had better go and visit the dentist in town as quickly as possible,' said Gwen.

'I can't,' sighed Miss Nicholson. 'I am taking the first formers for the next lesson. Not that I shall have much to do in the way of actual teaching, for I have set them an essay to write. But I daren't leave them to work unsupervised, for there are far too many scamps in that form!'

'If it is merely a matter of supervising them, surely I could do that,' said Gwen. 'Then you can pop into town and see the dentist.'

'I say, would you?' said Miss Nicholson, brightening. 'That would be awfully good of you. Just watch out for young Daffy Hope and her friend Katie, for they are always up to mischief.'

Then she handed Gwen a sheet of paper, and said, 'This is the essay I would like them to write. It should keep them safely occupied for the whole of the lesson.'

So, while Miss Nicholson went off to find Miss Potts, and explain that she had to rush off to see the dentist, Miss Lacey made her way to the first-form class-room.

The teacher was considerably softer-footed than Miss Nicholson, and the first formers did not hear her coming, so she walked into a scene of disarray. All of the first formers were chattering away like mad, Ivy and Edith were squabbling over possession of a ruler, and Daffy was standing on a chair, trying to attract the attention of someone outside the window.

For a moment, Miss Lacey wished that she had not made her generous offer to Miss Nicholson. The sixth formers were far too dignified and well-mannered to behave badly, but the first form was a very different kettle of fish. Then she pulled herself together, deciding that a few small girls certainly weren't going to get the better of Gwendoline Lacey!

'Girls!' she said, raising her voice. 'Quiet, please!'

Immediately the noise ceased, Daffy got down from her chair, and Ivy and Edith subsided.

Everyone stood, silently, and Miss Lacey, clearing her throat, said, 'Please sit down. Unfortunately, Miss Nicholson has had to go to the dentist, but she has left clear instructions for an essay that she wishes you to write.'

Daffy nudged Katie and whispered, 'Do you suppose that Miss Lacey will leave us to get on with it alone, or do you think that she will stay and supervise us?'

'Daffy!' said Miss Lacey sharply. 'Is there something you wish to say?'

'No, Miss Lacey,' said Daffy meekly, but with a glint of mischief in her eye.

'Then kindly keep quiet,' said the teacher, thinking how unlike her sister, Sally, the girl was. 'Now, you are to write an essay on the rivers of South America, which you may illustrate with maps, if you wish. Please get on with your work quickly and quietly, and if anyone wishes to ask anything, she must put her hand up.'

Though hopefully no one *would* ask anything, for Miss Lacey knew practically nothing about the rivers of South America!

Violet, watching the teacher closely, saw the flicker of uncertainty in her face, and smiled to herself. Amy didn't like Miss Lacey. And, because Amy didn't like her, Violet didn't like her either. How marvellous, she thought, if she could humiliate the teacher, and make her look small. Amy would be most impressed.

The girl wasn't brave enough to be openly rude to Miss Lacey, but halfway through the lesson, when they all had their heads down and were busily working away at their essays, Violet put her hand up and said, 'Miss Lacey, my pen has stopped working.'

'It probably needs some more ink,' said Miss Lacey, looking up.

'Oh no, for I filled it just before the lesson started,' said Violet, looking at her pen with a puzzled expression. 'I simply can't think what's the matter with it.'

'Well, you will have to borrow mine,' said Miss Lacey, rising and picking her pen up from the desk. 'But please make sure that you give it back to me at the end of the lesson, Violet.'

'Thank you, Miss Lacey,' said Violet demurely as the teacher walked towards her. 'I shall remember to give it back to you. I really don't understand why mine has suddenly decided to stop working, though!'

Then, as Miss Lacey leaned over to place the pen on her desk, Violet suddenly shook her own pen violently, and a shower of ink flew from it, leaving dark blue spots all over Miss Lacey's frilly white blouse.

'Oh!' cried the teacher, jumping backwards. 'Violet, you careless girl! Look what you have done. My blouse is quite ruined.'

Some of the first formers had to hide their mirth, for Miss Lacey really did look funny, standing there covered in ink.

'Miss Lacey, I'm so terribly sorry!' said Violet, looking and sounding most contrite, though the first formers had seen her smirk triumphantly. The teacher, however, hadn't, and she said, 'Oh well, I suppose accidents will happen. Now, I am putting you all on your honour to carry on with your essays and behave yourselves, while I go and get changed.'

'Yes, Miss Lacey,' chorused the first form.

But, of course, as soon as she was out of earshot, a perfect babble broke out.

'Violet, you did that on purpose!'

'Yes, you did, I saw the look on your face when the ink splattered Miss Lacey's blouse.'

'And your pen didn't stop working at all,' said Faith, who sat next to Violet. 'That was a fib. Why, Violet?'

'I know why!' said Daffy, suddenly. 'You're getting back at Miss Lacey because your precious Amy doesn't like her.'

'Violet, is that true?' gasped Faith, quite shocked.

'Of course it's true,' said Katie. 'Violet would do anything to score points with Amy. She already follows her around like a little puppy dog.'

'No, I don't!' said Violet hotly. 'Amy is my friend, and she enjoys my company. Why should any of you mind, anyway? At least I got Miss Lacey out of the room for a while.'

'I don't mind at all,' said Daffy with a shrug. 'Actually, I thought it was rather funny. But you are kidding yourself, Violet, if you think that Amy really sees you as a friend. Why on earth would a sixth former want to bother with a kid like you? She just enjoys having someone to worship her, that's all.'

Violet turned an angry red and, anxious to avert a quarrel, Faith said hastily, 'Miss Lacey is taking simply ages. I wonder where she has got to?'

'Perhaps she has gone to report Violet to Miss Potts,' suggested Edith slyly, grinning as Violet turned pale.

But Gwen hadn't done anything of the kind. Hurrying to her bedroom, so that she could change her clothes, she was spotted by Daisy.

'Good heavens, Miss Lacey!' cried the maid, looking at Gwen's ink-stained blouse in astonishment. 'Whatever has happened to you?'

'An accident,' sighed Gwen. 'Oh dear, I do hope that the ink will come out, for this is one of my favourite blouses.'

'Now, don't you worry about that, Miss,' said Daisy soothingly. 'I have something that will get the ink out in a trice. You go and get changed, then bring the blouse to me, and see if I don't have it looking as good as new for you.'

Then she peered closely at Gwen, and said, 'There's a little spot on your skirt, too, so I'd better have that as well. Once I've got the ink stains out, I'll wash and iron them for you, and you shall have them back in a few days.'

'Thanks awfully, Daisy,' said Gwen, sounding more cheerful. 'I really am most grateful.'

Of course, as soon as she had time, Violet rushed off to find Amy, and told her all about the incident.

Amy laughed, and patted Violet's golden head, saying, 'Well done, Violet. Oh, how I wish that I had been there to see that horrid Miss Lacey covered in ink!'

Violet giggled. The two of them were standing outside Amy's study, and the first former looked at the closed door with longing. She had never been invited into

Amy's study, and she would have so loved to go inside. Amy had such lovely things and such marvellous taste, Violet was quite certain that her study would be much nicer than any of the others. How thrilling it would be if Amy were to ask her in, so that they could sit and chat cosily together, perhaps over tea and biscuits. Violet would really feel that she had made a friend of Amy then.

Alas for such grand plans! Bonnie came along at that moment, and Amy said, 'Oh, there you are, Bonnie! I was just going to put the kettle on, and I have some delicious ginger biscuits that my grandmother sent. Will you join me?'

Bonnie accepted the invitation at once, and Violet continued to hang around, quite certain that Amy would ask her in for tea as well. But, instead, the sixth former turned to her, and said, 'You had better run along now, Violet. I daresay that your first-form friends will be wondering where you have got to.'

Violet was bitterly disappointed, and her mood was not improved when she spotted Edith coming out of Lizzie's study.

'It's all very well for Edith,' the girl thought, scowling. 'I bet she is always being invited into her sister's study for cosy chats.'

But Violet was quite wrong, for Edith had been summoned, rather than invited, and her chat with Lizzie had been far from cosy.

'I have come to a decision,' Lizzie had said heavily,

and Edith's heart had sank. Then it lifted again, as Lizzie said, 'I am going to give you a chance. I will turn a blind eye to the first-form feast and allow it to go ahead.'

'Oh, thank you, Lizzie!' said Edith, a smile lighting up her face. 'You won't regret it, I promise! We will be very careful, and –'

But Lizzie held up her hand, and said, 'I haven't finished yet, Edith. The feast can go ahead – provided that you give up any idea of taking part in the swimming gala.'

For a moment, Edith stared at her older sister as if she couldn't believe her ears. Then she cried, 'But you can't ask that of me, Lizzie! It's just not fair!'

'I'm sorry that you feel like that,' said Lizzie. 'But it is up to you to decide.'

'Well, I shan't!' said Edith, her cheeks flaming. 'You have no right to give me such an ultimatum, and I refuse to accept it. I *will* take part in the swimming gala! And if the first formers decide to hold their feast, you won't stop it!'

'I wouldn't be too sure of that, Edith,' said Lizzie, a hard look in her eyes. 'I shall be watching you all very carefully.'

Not trusting herself to say any more, Edith stalked from the room, resisting the impulse to slam the door behind her. Blow Lizzie! Why did she have to interfere all the time?

Then an idea came into her head, and she hurried off to find Daffy and Katie.

The two girls were in the courtyard, and Edith ran across to them.

'Hallo!' said Daffy. 'I say, whatever's up? You look awfully miserable!'

Quickly, Edith told the two girls of Lizzie's ultimatum, and they were quite outraged.

'Who does she think she is?'

'Thank goodness you stood up to her and told her what you thought!'

'Yes, but suppose Lizzie really does carry out her threat to stop our feast?' said Katie. 'Why, she could be sneaking on us to Miss Potts as we speak!'

'I don't think she would be foolish enough to do that,' said Daffy. 'She doesn't know when or where we are having the feast, so she wouldn't be able to give Miss Potts much information. Besides, Potty doesn't much care for sneaks and I think she might send Lizzie away with a flea in her ear.'

'And Potty can hardly punish us for *thinking* about having a feast,' said Edith. 'Why, even if she found our store of food, we could always say that we were planning a teatime party. No, Lizzie means to catch us in the act, then Miss Potts can't doubt her word.'

'Well, unless she stays up and sits outside our dormitory every night, I don't see how she *can* catch us out,' said Katie.

'That's the thing, though,' said Edith with a grimace. 'Lizzie is so persistent, and so used to having her own way, that she is quite likely to do just that!'

'Then what are we to do?' asked Daffy blankly.

'Well, that is where you and Katie come in,' said Edith. 'I'm going to throw Lizzie off the scent, and I want her to overhear the two of you talking about our feast on Sunday night. But I want you to say that we are having it by the pool, and going for a midnight swim too. If I know my sister, she will come outside well before midnight, and lie in wait for us.'

'So she will be out of the way when we leave the dormitory and have our feast indoors,' said Daffy thoughtfully. 'Which is all fine, but when we don't appear at the pool, she's sure to investigate. And she'll no doubt start by taking a look in at our dormitory, which will be empty!'

'Oh no, she won't!' said Edith grimly. 'I gave you my word that I would keep Lizzie out of the way, and I shall.'

'How?' asked Katie.

But Edith refused to tell, and would only say, 'The less you know about it the better.'

Daffy and Katie had the chance to put their plan into action that very evening as they strolled through the grounds before prep.

Coming round a corner, Daffy almost walked right into Lizzie, but the sixth former had her back turned, and didn't see the two first formers. Daffy swiftly retreated back round the corner and, winking at Katie, she raised her voice and said, 'My word, I can't wait until Sunday evening, Katie.'

'Nor can I,' said Katie eagerly. 'A midnight swim, followed by a picnic at the pool. It's going to be super.'

'Yes, we will have to come down at about a quarter to twelve, I should think,' said Daffy. 'For we shall need to get changed into our swimming costumes first.'

The two girls continued to chatter, talking in detail about the feast, but Lizzie, just around the corner, had heard enough. She knew all that she needed to, and now she hurried back to her study to make plans.

So, the first formers were holding their feast by the pool on Sunday night, were they? Well, they could jolly well think again! She, Lizzie, intended to find a good hiding place by the pool, and be there ready to surprise the first formers. The rules about girls leaving their tower at night were very strict indeed, and Miss Potts would take a dim view. A pang of conscience smote Lizzie then, for although she wanted to stop the feast, she didn't want to get her young sister into trouble. Or the other first formers, for that matter. But it was quite Edith's own fault for being so obstinate. If only she had agreed to give up her place in the swimming gala, the first form could have enjoyed their feast in peace. Lizzie still disapproved strongly of such things as midnight feasts, of course, but she had been prepared to compromise a little. In the long run, one late night was going to do less harm to Edith's studies than this swimming nonsense, which took up far too much of her time. Lizzie really did think that she had been very fair and reasonable in saying that the feast could go ahead, but her sister had thrown it back in her face. Miss Potts was sure to punish the first formers severely, but if it made Edith knuckle down, and realise that school wasn't all fun and games, it would be worth it.

Midnight feast

Lizzie told no one about her plans to sneak on the first formers, for she knew that the others would disapprove most strongly.

Alice, however, realised that the girl was preoccupied and did her best to find out what was troubling her.

'Oh, it's nothing,' said Lizzie, when Alice asked her what was wrong. 'I've just had a silly quarrel with Edith, that's all.'

But Alice watched Lizzie closely, and it seemed to her that there was more on her mind than just a silly quarrel. Lizzie did not confide in Alice, though, which was disappointing, for Alice had begun to feel that the two of them were growing closer since half-term.

As Sunday dawned, the first formers were very excited indeed about their feast.

'What a super day it's going to be,' said Ivy happily. 'No lessons, just a glorious day in the sun and a midnight feast to finish off with.'

But that afternoon a thought occurred to Katie as the first formers lazed on the grass, and she sat bolt upright.

'We don't have anything to drink!' she cried. 'I meant to get some bottles of ginger beer yesterday, but June called an extra tennis practice, so I didn't get the chance to go into town.'

'Blow!' said Faith. 'We simply must have something to drink.'

'I suppose we could drink water,' said Violet, wrinkling her nose. 'But it just won't be the same.'

'Water?' said Daffy, looking horrified. 'We can't possibly drink water at a midnight feast! No, I'm sure I can talk one of the kitchen staff into supplying us with something better.'

The first formers thought that this was a marvellous idea, for the angelic-looking Daffy was a great favourite with the kitchen staff. The girl leaped to her feet at once, and raced to the kitchen.

Cook wasn't there, but Daisy was, sitting at the big scrubbed table and drinking a cup of tea.

'Hallo, Daisy,' said Daffy. 'Sorry, I didn't mean to interrupt your break. Is Cookie about?'

'No, she's gone for a bit of a lie-down, for this heat doesn't agree with her,' said Daisy. 'Is there something I can do for you, Miss Daffy?'

Daffy hesitated, looking at the young maid. Then Daisy grinned, and Daffy saw the twinkle in her eye, and decided that she could be trusted.

'The thing is, Daisy,' said Daffy, shutting the kitchen door behind her. 'I wondered if there was any chance of you sparing a couple of jugs of lemonade for a little party that we first formers are planning tonight.'

'Oho!' said Daisy, with a knowing look. 'And would

this party happen to be taking place at midnight, Miss Daffy?'

'Yes,' admitted Daffy. 'But please don't tell anyone, Daisy, or it will all be spoiled.'

'You can trust me,' said Daisy, her grin broadening. 'There's no harm in you youngsters having a bit of fun, that's what I say. I shall leave two jugs of lemonade in here for you tonight, and I shan't say a word to anyone.'

'Thanks awfully, Daisy,' said Daffy happily. 'You're a good sort. I'll see if we can save you a piece of birthday cake!'

Then she went to report back to the others, and Katie said, 'Hooray for Daisy! Violet, you still haven't told us where we are having the feast.'

'All in good time,' said Violet airily. 'I shall tell you tonight.'

Violet had planned to go along to the housekeeper's room that evening and take the key from her room, but she had had an extraordinary piece of good luck. Earlier that day, she had passed the study that Miss Lacey and Miss Nicholson shared. The door was ajar, and Violet could see that it was empty. And there, on the desk, was the key to Miss Lacey's classroom! Violet hesitated. Dare she sneak in and grab it? It was Sunday, so Miss Lacey would not need to use the key today, and the chances were she would not even miss it. Quickly, before she could change her mind, Violet darted into the little study and snatched the key up from the desk, stuffing it into the pocket of her blazer before dashing out again. She felt horribly guilty, but it wasn't as if the first formers were going to leave the room in a mess. They would tidy up after themselves, then she, Violet, would find an opportunity to slip the key back on Miss Lacey's desk before she had even missed it.

Now, as she sat outside with the others, Violet patted the pocket of her blazer, feeling the key safely nestled inside. Oh, what a marvellous night this was going to be!

Lizzie had also made her plans. She intended to go to bed early, and was going to set her little alarm clock for quarter past eleven. That would give her time to dress and slip outside, so that she was there when the first formers came outside for their feast. She had found the perfect hiding place, for there was a small shed down by the pool, where life-belts and the like were stored. If she crouched down beside it, she had a clear view of the pool and the path leading down from the school. Oh, those first formers had a shock coming to them tonight!

Alice put her head round the door of Lizzie's study that evening and said, 'I was just about to have a mug of cocoa. Do you fancy joining me?'

'Thanks, Alice,' said Lizzie. 'But I was just about to turn in. I've got a bit of a headache, and I'm hoping that a good night's sleep will cure it.'

'I thought that you didn't seem yourself,' said Alice. 'Oh well, you get to bed then, and if you're no better tomorrow, perhaps you had better go along and see Matron.'

Lizzie promised that she would, but when she was alone once more, she sighed heavily. The girl had grown very fond of Alice, for she had proved to be a good friend – and now Lizzie had repaid her kindness by lying to her. But she would make it up to Alice somehow. The girl would receive her meagre pocket money from home in a day or two, and she vowed to spend every penny of it on treating Alice to tea in town, even though it meant that she would be broke for the remainder of the month. Her conscience slightly eased by this decision, Lizzie went up to bed, and was fast asleep when the others came up.

The first formers were only too keen to go to bed for once, and there were none of the usual groans and grumbles when the bell sounded.

'I am going to stay awake until eleven o'clock,' said Katie. 'Then I will wake Daffy, and she will sit up until midnight.'

'Then I will have the unenviable task of rousing the rest of you,' said Daffy wryly. 'Violet, I warn you, if you don't get out of bed as soon as I wake you, we will start the feast without you!'

'Don't worry, Daffy,' laughed Violet. 'I wouldn't miss this feast for the world!'

'Daffy, don't forget that you have to wake me before the others,' said Edith. 'I have to go and see what my dear sister is up to.'

'Oh, I almost forgot!' said Daffy. 'Thank goodness you reminded me. Edith, I do hope that your plan to keep Lizzie out of the way works. It will be too bad if you have to spend the whole night leading her on a wild goose chase, and miss the feast.'

'Don't worry, it will work, all right,' said Edith. 'But I can't join you others at the feast if I don't know where it is! Violet, do stop being mysterious and *tell* us!'

'Oh, very well,' said Violet rather grudgingly, for she had planned on keeping her secret until the very last second, and had pictured herself leading the others to Miss Lacey's classroom, and hearing their gasps of amazement as she produced the key and unlocked the door with a flourish.

So she was determined to extract every ounce of drama from the situation now, and, climbing out of bed, she reached into the pocket of her dressing-gown and produced a key, which she held up so that everyone could see it.

'This,' she announced, looking round at everyone, 'is the key to Miss Lacey's class-room. And that is where we are having our feast.'

There was a very mixed reaction indeed, for while some of the girls were thrilled at the thought of having their feast in the 'forbidden' class-room, others thought that Violet had gone too far.

'How exciting!'

'Oh, Violet, dare we?'

'Of course we dare! I've been simply dying to see inside that room.'

'Yes, but if we are caught we will get double the punishment you know!'

'Pooh! We shan't get caught.'

'Violet, do you mean to tell me that you took the key from the housekeeper's room?' asked Faith, looking quite horrified.

'Oh, no,' answered Violet, putting the key back in her pocket and climbing into bed again. 'I took it from Miss Lacey's study.'

Everyone stared at Violet in silence, then Daffy burst out laughing and said, 'I take my hat off to you, Violet! I didn't think you had it in you!'

'It's not funny!' said Faith severely. 'Violet, you have stolen Miss Lacey's property from her study.'

Violet looked rather taken aback at this, for she had not even considered that. Then she said stoutly, 'Nonsense! I haven't stolen it, merely borrowed it. I shall take it back as soon as I can, and she will be none the wiser.'

'I hope she won't, for your sake,' said Ivy.

There was a little more chat, and Miss Potts, making her way along the corridor outside, frowned as she heard the sound of voices coming from the dormitory. She put her hand on the doorknob, but before she turned it, Faith's clear voice came to her ears, saying, 'Quiet now, girls! Let's all try and get some sleep.'

Pleased, the mistress turned and walked away. Faith had turned out to be a very good head-girl, firm and fair. And it was just as well, for the first formers could be a little unruly at times, and they needed someone who was able to keep them in order.

Excited though they were, most of them fell asleep at

once, all except for Katie, of course. She had brought a book to bed with her, to while away the time, and she read it beneath the covers, with the aid of a torch. Even so, the time seemed to pass very slowly, and Katie felt her eyelids drooping several times. But at last it was eleven o'clock, and she padded across to shake the sleeping Daffy.

Daffy sat up at once, blinking a little and wondering why she was being woken in the middle of the night. Then she remembered – it was the night of the feast, and there was only one hour to go!

As Katie snuggled down in her own bed and dropped off to sleep, Daffy sat hugging her knees, her eyes shining in the darkness. She simply couldn't wait for midnight!

A short while later, Edith, who had only slept fitfully, began to stir. As she got out of bed and put her slippers on, Daffy whispered, 'Edith, do take care, won't you? Keep to the shadows, and make sure that none of the mistresses see you.'

'Don't worry about me,' Edith whispered back. 'I shan't get caught.'

And, quickly, the girl slipped on her dressing-gown and tiptoed softly from the room.

It took moments to reach the bottom of the stair, and let herself out of the side door that led into the garden. Then, heeding Daffy's advice, she kept to the shadows, making her way to the cliff path that led down to the pool.

The moon was very bright that night, and Edith hid

behind a large tree, looking all around. Everything seemed quiet and peaceful, with nothing to be seen. Then, suddenly, a small movement over by the old shed caught Edith's eye. Someone was hiding there, and that someone was Lizzie, she was certain of it!

But, before Edith could move, she suddenly saw another figure coming down the cliff path, and her heart leaped into her mouth. Could someone have followed her – and, if so, who?

Hardly daring to breathe, Edith flattened herself against the broad trunk of the tree as the figure drew closer. Then it walked straight past, without having spotted Edith, and the girl let out a little sigh of relief. Edith peered round the trunk of the tree, and saw that the mysterious person was making her way to the shed. Then she frowned. There was something awfully familiar about the person, the way that she walked, her clothes . . . Edith gave a gasp as she realised who it was. Miss Lacey! But what on earth was she doing out here at this time of night?

Lizzie, hiding beside the shed, also watched Miss Lacey approaching, and didn't quite know what to do. Should she make her presence known, and tell the mistress that she was waiting to catch the first formers out? Or should she simply keep quiet and wait to see if Miss Lacey went away?

Alas for Lizzie, she had no choice in the matter, for all of a sudden she felt a terrific tickle in her nose and, quite without warning, she sneezed suddenly.

Miss Lacey, almost at the door of the shed, stopped dead in her tracks, and looked in the direction from where the sneeze had come. Of course, she spotted Lizzie at once, and gave a gasp.

Caught out, Lizzie could do nothing but stand up, and stammer, 'M-Miss Lacey, I daresay you wonder what I am doing here at this hour. The thing is, you see –'

But she got no further, for Miss Lacey suddenly put a warning finger to her lips, and beckoned Lizzie forward.

How odd, thought Lizzie, moving to Miss Lacey's side. The teacher was wearing a hat with a little veil, which covered the top part of her face. What a very strange thing to wear for a late-night stroll in the grounds.

'I thought I heard a noise in the shed,' whispered Miss Lacey, her voice sounding rather hoarse and strained. 'Lizzie, open the door and take a look.'

Lizzie hadn't heard a sound, and said, 'There can't be anything or anyone in the shed, Miss Lacey, for the door is locked from the outside. See? The key is still in the keyhole.'

'I tell you, I heard something,' insisted Miss Lacey, still in the same hoarse voice. 'Open the door at once. '

So Lizzie turned the key and pulled open the door, wrinkling her nose at the musty smell that came from the old shed. It was very dark and gloomy in there, and Lizzie could hardly see a thing as she poked her head inside.

Then, suddenly, she felt a hand between her shoulder blades, propelling her forwards, and she was thrust into the shed, only just managing to keep her balance as the door was pushed shut behind her.

'Miss Lacey!' cried poor Lizzie as she heard the key turning in the lock. 'Miss Lacey, let me out at once!'

Bewildered, angry and a little frightened, Lizzie beat at the door with her fists, but the mistress did not answer. Poor Lizzie did not even know if she was still there, or if she had gone away.

Edith, who had watched the whole astonishing scene from a safe distance, ducked down behind a hedge as Miss Lacey walked back up the cliff path and went towards the school. Then, once the mistress was out of sight, she stood up and looked towards the shed, from which she could hear Lizzie's faint cries.

The girl didn't have the slightest idea why Miss Lacey had imprisoned Lizzie, and she supposed she really ought to go and let her sister out. But the fact was Miss Lacey had done exactly what she, Edith, had planned to do herself! The first former had been quite determined not to let her older sister spoil the feast, and she had decided to somehow lure her to the shed, then lock her in.

Oh dear, thought Edith, as she stood at the bottom of the cliff path, wringing her hands. What a dreadful dilemma! It was one thing for her to lock Lizzie up, to prevent her from ruining the feast. But it was quite another for Miss Lacey to do it, for her own mysterious purposes! In fact, it was quite dreadful. Whoever heard of a mistress doing such a thing? And what on earth could Miss Lacey be up to? But Edith had no time to ponder that now, for the others would be wondering what had happened to her. She gave a last, regretful look over her shoulder at the shed as she walked up the cliff path. It was most unfortunate, but it wouldn't do Lizzie any real harm to spend an hour or so in the shed, and Edith would make sure that she was released once the feast was over. Perhaps, thought the girl, it might even teach her a lesson, and she would think twice before spying on the first formers in future!

A most dramatic night

'I wonder where Edith has got to?' said Faith rather worriedly as the first formers finished setting out the food on the big table in Miss Lacey's class-room.

'I daresay she will be here at any moment,' said Ivy. 'Do try not to fret, Faith.'

'Isn't it marvellous to be able to have our feast in such splendour?' said Daffy. 'And to set the food out on the table, rather than the floor, and sit on chairs to eat.'

'Yes, you've done us proud, Violet,' said Katie, clapping the girl on the shoulder. 'What gave you the idea of using this room?'

Violet had meant to keep her visit to the room with Amy a secret but, basking in the others' praise, she couldn't resist boasting a little.

'Amy brought me in here once,' she said. 'Of course, you mustn't say a word to anyone else, for the other sixth formers are so stuffy that I don't suppose they would like it at all if they knew that Amy had let me into their precious drawing-room.'

'I should think they would be furious with her,' said Faith, staring at Violet in wonder. 'Amy really is the limit!'

Violet was about to leap to Amy's defence, but suddenly Daffy hissed, 'Hush! I can hear footsteps outside.'

As the others fell silent, they could hear the footsteps too, then they froze as the door was pushed open.

Everyone groaned with relief as they realised that it was Edith who stood there, a smile on her face.

'Don't stand there grinning like an idiot!' said Daffy, grabbing her arm and pulling her into the room. 'Let's get this door shut, before anyone sees the light.'

'Was Lizzie lying in wait for us?' asked Katie anxiously. 'Did you manage to get rid of her?'

'I can promise that Lizze won't be sneaking on us tonight,' said Edith, quite truthfully.

She would have dearly loved to tell the others of the strange events that had taken place by the swimming-pool, but one or two of the girls might feel a little uneasy if they knew that poor Lizzie was imprisoned in a shed! It would ruin things if Faith decided to go and let her out! They might also feel uncomfortable if they knew that Miss Lacey was on the prowl.

Edith had kept a wary eye out for the mistress as she walked back to the school, but there had been no sign of Miss Lacey. At one point, Edith had felt sure that she was being followed, but, glancing nervously over her shoulder, she had been relieved to see that no one was there, and had hurried back indoors as fast as she could.

Then she put Miss Lacey to the back of her mind, for there was no way that she could have heard about the first formers' feast, so Edith felt quite certain that, whatever the mistress was doing, she wasn't out to make trouble for them. All the same, she turned to Violet, and said, 'It might be an idea to lock the door. That way if anyone does come prowling around, they won't be able to get in.'

'Good idea,' said Violet, going across and doing just that.

'And, now that we are all settled,' said Daffy, 'let the feast begin!'

The girls sat round the big table and tucked in, feasting on tinned prawns and sardines, pork pie and sausage rolls. Then there were ripe, juicy strawberries, biscuits, chocolate – and a simply enormous birthday cake, which Ivy and Katie had bought between them.

'It's so beautiful that it's almost a shame to cut it,' said Faith, looking at the pink and yellow sugar roses that decorated the cake.

'We'll have to cut it if we are to enjoy it,' said the ever-practical Ivy, beginning to slice the cake. 'Help yourselves, everyone, with good wishes from Katie and me.'

'Happy birthday to you both!' chorused the girls as they raised glasses full of lemonade.

'Yes, even though yours was yesterday, Katie,' said Daffy.

'And mine isn't until tomorrow,' said Ivy.

'No, it is after midnight,' pointed out Violet. 'So your birthday is today.'

'So it is!' said Ivy happily, taking a sip of lemonade. 'Well, this is a jolly good start to it, I must say.'

'What a super night this is,' said Faith with a contented sigh. 'I really don't think that anything could spoil it.'

But she was wrong. Something could – and something was just about to!

Miss Potts was roused from a deep sleep shortly after one o'clock. She sat up and switched on her bedside lamp, wondering what it could have been that had woken her so suddenly. There were no strange noises to be heard, but *something* had disturbed her, so the mistress put on her glasses, which were on the bedside table, and went to look out of her window. It was a perfectly still summer night, with no wind and no rain, and there was nothing to be seen outside. Puzzled, the mistress had just decided to go back to bed, when a floorboard creaked outside her room, and there came a sharp rapping at her door.

Miss Potts jumped, and went across to the door, pulling it open. But there was no one to be seen there, either. How very odd! Miss Potts looked along the corridor, just in time to see a figure disappearing round the corner. Who it was she didn't know, for she only had the briefest glimpse. But whoever it was must be the person who had knocked on her door.

Most annoyed at being disturbed, the mistress quickly put on her dressing-gown and slippers, before setting off in pursuit of the culprit. It was probably one of the younger girls, dared by another to play a prank. But Miss Potts did not care for pranks, especially in the middle of the night, and woe betide the girl when she caught up with her!

The mistress went round the corner where she had seen the figure disappearing. And now she seemed to have vanished completely, for there was no sign of her – how annoying! But then Miss Potts peered over the banisters, just in time to see someone going towards Miss Lacey's class-room, and she made her way quickly down the stairs.

Now Miss Potts was in luck, for when she reached the corridor where the class-room was, the person was standing right outside, as if wondering whether to go in. Why, it was Miss Lacey! But what on earth was she doing wandering round the school at this late hour? Miss Potts wondered if she could be sleepwalking, but no, she was fully dressed – why, she was even wearing a hat!

'Miss Lacey!' hissed Miss Potts in a low voice, for although they were away from any bedrooms and dormitories, she didn't want to risk disturbing anyone.

Miss Lacey turned sharply and, for a moment, Miss Potts thought that she was going to say something. But then she scuttled away down the corridor, leaving Miss Potts feeling most exasperated. What on *earth* was she playing at?

The mistress was about to follow, when she heard a sound coming from the class-room. The unmistakable sound of girls giggling. She pursed her lips. Really, the whole school seemed to have gone quite mad tonight!

The first formers, busily clearing away after their feast, hadn't heard anything at all outside. So it came as a terrible shock to them when someone tried the handle of the door.

Katie dropped the plate that she was holding, and the thud it made as it landed on the carpet sounded very loud indeed in the still of the night.

'Idiot!' hissed Ivy, giving her a push.

'Hush!' whispered Faith. 'Let's try to keep calm until we know who is there.'

Then Miss Potts knocked smartly on the door, making everyone jump again.

'Who do you think it is?' whispered Violet fearfully, clutching at Daffy's arm.

'I don't know,' Daffy whispered back, trying to sound brave. 'But whoever it is, it means trouble for us!'

Then Miss Potts spoke, sounding very angry indeed. 'I know that there is someone in there, and I insist that you open this door at once!'

'Oh, help, it's Potty!' groaned Edith. 'Now what are we to do?'

'There's only one thing we can do,' sighed Faith. 'Open the door and face the consequences. Blow!'

'Your sister must have sneaked, after all,' said Ivy, to Edith, looking cross.

'She didn't,' said Edith shortly. 'Whoever told Miss Potts that we were in here, I can assure you that it wasn't Lizzie.'

Faith, meanwhile, had unlocked the door, with trembling hands, and now she opened it and stood aside to let Miss Potts in.

At once, everyone fell silent, their heads bent and eyes downcast, as Miss Potts's keen eyes took in the remnants of the feast and she saw at a glance what had been going on.

'Well!' she said in a stern voice. 'Not content with breaking one school rule by holding a midnight feast, you have broken another by holding it in a room that is out of bounds. Have you anything to say for yourselves?'

As head of the form, Faith stepped forward and said, 'We are awfully sorry, Miss Potts. But you see, it was Katie's birthday, then Ivy's, and –'

'And you thought that was a reasonable excuse to flout the rules,' said Miss Potts scornfully. 'I am very disappointed in you all.'

The girls hung their heads, then Miss Potts said, 'How did you manage to get hold of a key to this room? I suppose that you took it from the housekeeper's room?'

There was a long silence, and Violet's knees began to tremble.

'Well?' said Miss Potts sharply. 'I am waiting for an answer.'

'You'll have to own up, Violet,' whispered Daffy. 'It can't be helped.'

So, feeling quite faint, Violet said, in a shaking voice, 'I took the key from Miss Lacey's study, Miss Potts.'

The mistress stared at Violet incredulously. Then she said, 'This just becomes more and more serious! Well, it is too late to deal with you now. Go back to bed, all of you, and report to Miss Grayling's office immediately after breakfast tomorrow.'

'But, Miss Potts, we haven't finished clearing up,' ventured Daffy in a small voice.

'You will give up your break and do it tomorrow,' said Miss Potts severely. 'And see that you make a good job of it! Now, off to bed with you at once. Edith, why are you standing rooted to the spot?'

'You see, Miss Potts,' said Edith hesitantly. 'There is something else. My sister, Lizzie, is locked in the shed down by the swimming-pool, and I really think that someone should go and let her out.'

Miss Potts stared at Edith as if she couldn't believe her ears! Had her form taken leave of their senses tonight?

The first formers looked at one another in surprise too, for it was the first they had heard of Lizzie being locked in the shed!

'Am I to understand, Edith, that you locked your sister in a shed?' asked Miss Potts in a carefully controlled tone.

'Oh no, Miss Potts,' said Edith, shaking her head. 'It wasn't me. I meant to, for I knew that she intended to spoil our feast but, as things turned out, I didn't need to. You see, it was Miss Lacey who locked her in. I saw her.'

For a moment, Miss Potts wondered if Edith was

being foolish enough to try to make a joke. Then she looked at the girl's earnest expression, and realised that she was serious.

Faintly, the mistress said, 'Miss Lacey locked Lizzie in the shed.'

'That's right, Miss Potts,' said Edith. 'I know it sounds quite incredible, but please believe me, for it's the truth.'

Well, Miss Lacey had certainly been behaving very strangely a little while ago, thought Miss Potts, on whom the evening's events were beginning to take their toll. Perhaps she had taken leave of her senses, and really *had* imprisoned Lizzie.

'Very well,' she said wearily. 'Edith, you come with me to the swimming-pool, and the rest of you get to bed.'

'Yes, Miss Potts,' chorused the girls, sounding very subdued.

'And if there is one more sound from your dormitory tonight, whatever punishment Miss Grayling gives you tomorrow will be increased ten-fold,' she said firmly. 'Violet, please give me the key to this room, so that I can lock the door when everyone has left.'

Meekly, Violet handed over the key, and everyone left the room, the first formers trooping silently back to their dormitory, while Miss Potts and Edith made their way down to the pool.

There wasn't a sound coming from the shed, and Edith wondered if her sister had fallen asleep in there. Not that it would be a terribly comfortable place to sleep, for there was only a hard floor, and Edith wouldn't be at all surprised if there were spiders in there – and Lizzie simply hated spiders. Her conscience, which had been troubling her a little all night, now came fully alive. Poor Lizzie must have suffered quite an ordeal.

Miss Potts was turning the key in the padlock and, as she opened the door, Edith gave a cry – for the shed was quite empty! But how on earth could Lizzie have escaped, for there wasn't so much as a small window in the shed. Or had Miss Lacey returned and let her out?

Miss Potts turned her stern gaze upon Edith, who said hastily, 'Miss Potts, Lizzie really was locked in the shed, you must believe me!'

Miss Potts did, for it was quite obvious that the girl was telling the truth, and she said wearily, 'Well, she is not there now. Hopefully she is safely asleep in her dormitory. I shall go and check on my way back to bed. I trust that, in the morning, we will get to the bottom of all these strange events.'

Miss Potts escorted Edith back to her dormitory, then went to see if Lizzie was in her bed. Fortunately, the girl was, fast asleep and looking none the worse for her ordeal. Miss Potts was pleased, for she really felt quite exhausted now and didn't think that she could deal with any more extraordinary events that evening. But there was still one more thing that she had to do before she could finally retire. On the way to her own bedroom, the mistress stopped outside Miss Lacey's room and, very quietly and carefully, she pushed open the door.

Miss Lacey lay in bed, breathing deeply, her eyes

closed, and her clothes hung neatly over the back of a chair. That was odd, thought Miss Potts, frowning, for they weren't the clothes that Miss Lacey had been wearing a little while ago. But she was too relieved that the teacher had ceased her nocturnal wandering to worry about that now. Closing the door softly behind her, Miss Potts went back to her own bedroom and fell into an exhausted sleep, where she dreamed of midnight feasts, girls locked in sheds and sinister, shadowy figures who roamed the corridors at night!

Miss Lacey's strange behaviour

In fact, Lizzie had been released from her prison by Felicity and Alice.

Alice had been woken by a ray of moonlight coming in through a chink in the curtains. When she had got up to close the curtains properly, she had seen that Lizzie's bed was empty. Oh well, the girl had thought, perhaps she had just gone to get a glass of water, for it was a very warm evening. But, when Lizzie did not return, she began to feel a little uneasy, and decided that she had better go and look for the girl.

As she was donning her slippers and dressing-gown, a voice in the darkness whispered, 'Alice, is that you? What are you doing?'

'Oh, Felicity,' whispered Alice. 'Lizzie isn't in her bed, and I'm going to look for her. I'm a little worried, because I think she has had something on her mind the last few days.'

'Well, you can't possibly go wandering round on your own,' Felicity said, sitting up. 'I'll come with you. Go to my bedside cabinet, Alice, and you'll find a torch there. We'll take that with us.'

Soon the two girls found themselves at the little side

door, through which Edith had let herself out earlier. But, on letting herself back in again, Edith had been in such a hurry that she hadn't closed it properly, and now it stood ajar.

'This is very odd,' said Felicity, with a frown. 'The maids are usually so thorough about locking up at night.'

'I wonder if Lizzie could have let herself out though this door?' said Alice. 'But whatever can she be doing outside?'

'I don't know,' said Felicity. 'But we had better try to find her quickly.'

The girls' search eventually took them to the cliff path that led to the swimming-pool and, as they walked down it, Alice stopped suddenly, grasping Felicity's arm.

'Did you hear that?' she said. 'It sounded like somebody yelling. Listen! There it is again!'

'Yes, I heard it that time,' said Felicity. 'It seems to be coming from that shed. Come on, Alice, let's go and investigate.'

Lizzie could have almost wept with relief when she heard the voices of the two girls outside her prison, and she fell into Alice's arms as the door was opened.

'Lizzie!' cried Felicity in astonishment. 'What on earth happened?'

'She's frozen,' said Alice, chafing the girl's hands.

Indeed, Lizzie was shivering dreadfully, for although it had been warm earlier, the night had turned very chilly, and the dark little shed was cold.

'Let's go back to my study,' said Felicity. 'I'll make us all some hot cocoa, then Lizzie can get warm.'

The thought of hot cocoa was very welcome indeed to Lizzie, but she said, 'I must go and find Miss Potts first. You see, the first formers are having a midnight feast.'

'Do you mean to tell me it was one of those little first-form wretches who locked you in here?' said Alice angrily.

'No,' said Lizzie. 'It was Miss Lacey, though why she should have done such a thing beats me.'

Felicity and Alice exchanged glances, for Lizzie didn't seem to be making any sense at all.

'Lizzie, you are coming back to my study for a hot drink, and that's an order,' said Felicity firmly. 'Then you can tell Alice and me exactly what happened.'

Lizzie protested, but Felicity and Alice resolutely bore her up the cliff path and into school.

'Well,' said Alice, when the three of them were comfortably settled with mugs of hot cocoa. 'What's all this about, Lizzie?'

Lizzie told them the whole story, the two girls frowning in disapproval when she related how she had been lying in wait for the first formers to begin their feast. And when she told them that Miss Lacey had pushed her into the shed, their eyes grew wide with astonishment.

'Either you got hold of the wrong end of the stick, or the first formers were having you on,' said Felicity, when she had finished. 'There was no feast going on at the pool tonight, that much was obvious.'

'I know that they are having a feast,' said Lizzie stubbornly. 'Edith as good as told me so when I caught her hiding some food she had bought.'

'Well, what if they were?' said Alice. 'Goodness me, there's no harm in an occasional midnight feast! What a spoilsport you are, Lizzie.'

Lizzie turned red and said, rather stiffly, 'I think that there is a great deal of harm in it. Edith should be concentrating on her studies, not on pranks and feasts.'

'Lizzie, you really have got a bee in your bonnet about all this,' said Felicity, frowning at the girl. 'Midnight feasts are part and parcel of boarding school life. Yes, they are against the rules. But this is a rule that all schoolgirls break at some time or other, for it is just a bit of harmless fun.'

'Oh, you don't understand!' said Lizzie, becoming agitated. 'If Edith gets into trouble, or doesn't do well here, it could mean no more Malory Towers for both of us.'

'Whatever do you mean?' said Alice curiously. 'I say, Lizzie, this isn't something to do with that uncle of yours, is it?'

'What uncle?' said Felicity. Then she saw that Lizzie was looking uncomfortable, and said, 'Look here, Lizzie, if there's something you want to get off your chest, you may be sure that neither Alice nor I will betray your confidence. Isn't that so, Alice?'

Alice nodded emphatically and, at last, Lizzie said, 'As I told you, Alice, our uncle pays our school fees. But what I didn't tell you is that he expects Edith and me to repay him, once we are old enough and are making our way in the world.'

Neither Felicity nor Alice knew quite what to say to this, and Lizzie went on, 'Mother impressed on us that we had to work hard and pass all our exams well, for that is the only way that we will be able to get good jobs and pay Uncle Charles back when we are older. If he thinks either of us is wasting our time here, there is a good chance that he will refuse to continue paying the fees, then Edith and I will have to leave, and I will probably have to go out and find a job. But I know that I shall be able to get a much better one if I finish my education first.'

'Well, I see now why studying is so important to you,' said Felicity, frowning. 'And why you are so hard on young Edith at times. But I'm sure that your uncle wants you both to have fun here too, and be able to look back upon your time at Malory Towers with enjoyment.'

'Perhaps,' said Lizzie. 'You see, neither of us know Uncle Charles awfully well. He is Father's older brother, and he lives a long way from us, so we never see very much of him.'

'Personally, I always found it easier to study if I had a little fun and relaxation in between,' said Alice. 'You sort of come back to it with a fresh mind then, whereas if you sit poring over a book for hours on end, everything ends up getting all muddled in your mind. At least, it does in *my* mind.'

'Yes, I suppose you are right,' said Lizzie thoughtfully. Then she sighed, and said, 'I wonder where Edith and her friends are holding their feast tonight? I overheard Daffy and Katie talking about it, and distinctly heard them say that it was tonight, by the swimming-pool.'

'They probably knew that you were listening, and were leading you up the garden path,' said Alice drily.

'I wouldn't be at all surprised,' said Felicity. 'I must say, I'm much more concerned about Miss Lacey's part in this than anything the youngsters might be up to. Lizzie, are you absolutely certain that she was the one who locked you in the shed?'

'Absolutely,' said Lizzie firmly. 'She was acting awfully strange, and even her voice seemed peculiar – sort of hoarse.'

'You know that you will have to report it to Miss Grayling,' Felicity said soberly. 'And she will have to decide what is to be done, though I can't imagine her wanting to keep a mistress at Malory Towers who goes around locking up the pupils!'

'It's been a jolly odd sort of night,' said Alice, putting a hand up to her mouth to stifle a yawn. 'And now I suppose that we had better turn in, or we shall never be able to get up in the morning.'

The three girls made their way back to their dormitory, letting themselves in very quietly, so as not to disturb the others.

Alice and Lizzie fell asleep at once, but Felicity lay awake for a little while, puzzling over the evening's events, and Miss Lacey's part in them in particular.

'I remember Darrell saying that Gwen could be sly, and that she played some mean tricks on Mary-Lou when she was in the first form,' thought Felicity. 'But surely she has grown out of that kind of spiteful behaviour now? And what possible reason could she have for locking Lizzie in the shed?'

But Felicity couldn't come up with any reason at all for the mistress's extraordinary behaviour and, at last, she fell asleep too.

'Come on, sleepyheads!' said Susan, the following morning, as Felicity, Alice and Lizzie had great difficulty in getting out of bed. 'Anyone would think that the three of you had been up all night at a midnight feast, or something.'

'Nothing so jolly,' said Felicity, sighing as she left the comfort of her bed. 'Though we did have rather a disturbed night.'

'Do tell!' said Nora, who was standing in front of a mirror, brushing her hair.

So, with much prompting from Lizzie and Alice, Felicity told the sixth formers what had taken place last night. The others were very shocked and surprised, of course.

'Well! How very strange!'

'I've heard of girls playing pranks on teachers, but never teachers playing pranks on girls!'

'I would never have thought Miss Lacey capable of such a thing!'

'It doesn't surprise me in the slightest,' said Amy with a sniff. 'I always thought there was something rather odd about her.'

'Well, I think that Miss Lacey deserves a great big pat on the back,' declared June, giving Lizzie a scornful look. 'For she saved the first formers from having their feast ruined. You might call it looking out for your young sister, Lizzie, but as far as I'm concerned, you're no better than a sneak.'

Lizzie turned red, and Pam said hastily, 'My word, I wouldn't like to be in Miss Lacey's shoes when Miss Grayling hears about this. I wouldn't be a bit surprised if she is dismissed immediately.'

In fact, Miss Grayling already knew about Miss Lacey's behaviour, for Miss Potts had gone to the Head's study as soon as she was dressed and reported it.

'This is a very grave accusation, Miss Potts,' said Miss Grayling, looking at the mistress with a serious expression. 'You are quite certain that the person you saw in the corridor was Miss Lacey?'

'It certainly looked like her,' said Miss Potts. 'Edith actually saw her push Lizzie into the shed and lock the door. Apparently Miss Lacey spoke to Lizzie before she locked her in, though Edith was too far away to hear what she said. I haven't spoken to Lizzie myself yet, Miss Grayling, for I thought that you would want to do that.'

'Yes, and I will certainly need to see Miss Lacey,' said

the Head. 'That is not likely to be a pleasant interview, for if it is true that she imprisoned one of the girls I have no alternative but to send her away.'

'No, I don't suppose that you do,' said Miss Potts with a sigh. 'It is a great pity, though, for while I never had much time for Gwen when she was a pupil here, I was beginning to think that she had changed her ways and was actually making a go of things as a mistress.'

'Yes, so was I,' said Miss Grayling. 'How very disappointing it is to know that we were wrong! Miss Potts, send Miss Lacey to me at once, would you? I don't want her going into breakfast with the girls, for she must stay away from them until this matter has been resolved one way or another.'

'Of course, Miss Grayling,' said Miss Potts. Then she went off to knock on the door of Miss Lacey's bedroom.

The young mistress opened it, looking rather taken aback to see Miss Potts standing there at such an early hour. But she did not appear at all embarrassed or awkward, which, thought Miss Potts, was very odd, considering her strange behaviour of the night before.

'Miss Grayling would like to see you in her study at once, Miss Lacey,' Miss Potts said briskly.

'Before breakfast?' said Miss Lacey, sounding most surprised. 'Why, whatever does she want that is so urgent?'

'She will no doubt tell you that herself,' said Miss Potts. 'But I shouldn't keep her waiting if I were you, Miss Lacey.'

In the first-form dormitory, meanwhile, an air of gloom prevailed. All of the girls felt very tired indeed, and they had what was sure to be a pretty severe punishment to look forward to. Not even the fact that it was Ivy's birthday could cheer them up.

'I know it's got off to a rotten start,' said Katie dispiritedly, 'but happy birthday, Ivy, old girl.'

'Thanks,' said Ivy, doing her best to conjure up a smile. 'Oh well, at least things can only get better.'

And, for a while, things did get a little better, as the girls all gave Ivy presents and cards.

'You're all very decent,' said Ivy. 'This almost makes up for being caught out last night.'

Just then, like a small whirlwind, Daffy burst in and cried, 'I say, you'll never guess what I've just heard! Apparently it was Miss Lacey who split on us to Miss Potts. I just overheard Potty discussing it with Matron outside the bathroom, and it seems that Miss Lacey led Miss Potts right to our door.'

'How mean of her!' cried Violet. 'We weren't doing any harm. Amy was quite right about her.'

'But how did she know that we were having a feast?' said Ivy, wrinkling her brow.

'She probably just found out by chance,' said Edith. 'She was certainly prowling around last night, for she shut Lizzie in the shed, remember. She must have come along this corridor and heard the noise we were making.'

'It's all very strange,' said Katie. 'I wonder why she *did* shut Lizzie in the shed?'

'I can't imagine,' said Edith. 'I just hope that Miss Grayling gets to the bottom of it, and that she sends Miss Lacey away as soon as possible.'

Miss Nicholson saves the day

It was a very trying day for Miss Grayling, and one that was full of surprises.

When Miss Lacey came to her study, the Head wasted no time at all in getting to the point.

The mistress was most astonished to discover that she had been accused of imprisoning Lizzie Mannering, and she protested her innocence hotly. Miss Grayling watched her closely, and had to admit that, if Miss Lacey was lying, she was a remarkably good actress.

'But Miss Potts saw you as well,' said Miss Grayling. 'You led her to your class-room, where the first formers were having a midnight feast.'

'They were holding a feast in my class-room?' gasped Miss Lacey. 'I knew nothing at all of this, Miss Grayling, you must believe me. And I certainly wasn't wandering around last night, either in the corridors or down by the pool.'

The Head hardly knew what to say, for there were three witnesses who swore that they had seen Miss Lacey last night, yet the young woman seemed very sincere in her protestations of innocence.

Just then, someone knocked urgently at the door,

and Miss Grayling called out, 'Come in.'

Miss Nicholson entered the room and, not at all pleased at being interrupted, the Head said, 'Miss Nicholson, I am rather busy at the moment. Could you come back later, please?'

'I'm awfully sorry to interrupt,' said Miss Nicholson. 'But, you see, Miss Grayling, I know what Miss Lacey has been accused of, for the story is all over the school.'

'Well, I suppose it was only a matter of time before gossip began to spread,' said Miss Grayling. 'But I fail to see how it concerns you, Miss Nicholson.'

'Oh, but it does!' said the mistress. 'You see, Miss Grayling, Miss Lacey was with me last night. We sat up until very late in our study, chatting away about all sorts of things. Isn't that so, Miss Lacey?'

Catching the meaningful expression on her friend's face, Miss Lacey nodded and said, 'Er – yes, it is just as Miss Nicholson says.'

'Well!' said the Head, looking surprised. 'This puts a very different complexion on things. It seems that the person seen wandering around Malory Towers last night must have been someone else. Though how she came to be wearing your clothes is quite a puzzle!'

'Miss Grayling,' said Miss Lacey. 'What was the person wearing?'

'A white blouse and pink floral patterned skirt, according to Miss Potts,' said the Head. 'And, most unusually, a hat with a small veil.'

'Well, I certainly have an outfit like that,' said Miss

Lacey, frowning. 'But Daisy took the skirt and blouse off to be cleaned, because Violet accidentally splashed ink on them, and I haven't had them back yet. As for the hat – well, now that I come to think about it, I haven't seen it for a while.'

'This just becomes more and more mysterious!' exclaimed the Head. 'I shall have to speak to Daisy about the clothes, of course. Miss Lacey, you may go, and I am very sorry that you were unjustly accused. Oh, and you had better have this back, too.'

The Head took something from her drawer, and handed it to Miss Lacey. It was the key to her class-room.

'Miss Potts gave me this,' said Miss Grayling. 'It seems that Violet took it from your study yesterday. Needless to say, she will be punished for it.'

Well, really, thought Miss Lacey, it was just one thing after another! Murmuring a faint word of thanks, she took the key and put it in her pocket. Then she and Miss Nicholson went on their way, walking along the corridor in silence, each of them lost in her own thoughts. Only when they were safely in their own study, with the door shut behind them, did Miss Lacey break the silence, saying, 'You told the Head a lie to get me out of trouble. Why did you do that?'

Miss Nicholson turned a little red, and said gruffly, 'Because you are my friend, and I know that you didn't do what you were accused of. If it had just been Lizzie's or Edith's word against yours, the Head might have believed you. But Miss Potts also thinks she saw you, and you know how much Miss Grayling trusts her.'

Gwen looked at Miss Nicholson's round, rather plain face, and suddenly knew the meaning of true friendship. She thought back over the girls she had tried to befriend during her time as a pupil at Malory Towers, and then at finishing school. All of them had been wealthy, gifted or beautiful. Miss Nicholson was none of these things, but she was kind, loyal and good-hearted. And those were the things that really mattered in a friend. Gwen had been stupid not to see it years ago, she realised now.

'Thanks awfully,' she said in a low voice. 'I'll never forget what you did for me today.'

'Oh, think nothing of it,' said Miss Nicholson, going back to her usual hearty manner. 'What we have to consider now is that there is someone going around disguised as you.'

'Yes, and whoever it is is causing trouble in the hope that I will get the blame,' said Gwen, frowning. 'How I wish I knew who it was!'

Miss Nicholson said nothing, apparently lost in thought, then, abruptly, she said, 'You never told me about the incident with Violet and the ink.'

Gwen shrugged. 'It hardly seemed worth mentioning. I was a little annoyed at the time, but it was just an accident and there was no real harm done.'

'Are you quite sure that it was an accident?' asked Miss Nicholson.

'I think so,' said Gwen, puzzled. 'Why do you ask?'

'Because it suddenly occurred to me that young Violet

positively worships Amy of the sixth form, and would do anything for her,' said Miss Nicholson. 'And Amy's dislike of you is well-known.'

'What are you getting at?' asked Gwen, her brow furrowed.

'Well, Amy is about the same height as you, though a little slimmer,' said Miss Nicholson. 'And her hair is the same colour, so . . .'

As Miss Nicholson's voice tailed off, light suddenly dawned on Gwen. 'You think it was *Amy* who was masquerading as me last night!' she gasped. 'Oh, my goodness!'

Just then the two mistresses heard someone humming a tune in the corridor outside, and Miss Nicholson said, 'That's Daisy! She always hums while she works. Let's see if she can shed any light on who may have taken your clothes.'

She pulled open the door, calling, 'Daisy, would you come in here for a moment, please?'

Daisy entered the study, looking a little scared, and Gwen said, 'Daisy, what happened to the skirt and blouse that I gave you to wash for me the other day? I haven't had them back yet.'

'Why, Miss Lacey, I washed and ironed them, just as I said I would,' said Daisy. 'And I went to hang them up in your bedroom, but the door was locked, so I brought them in here. In fact, I hung them over the back of that very chair that you are sitting on, Miss Lacey.'

The two mistresses exchanged glances, and Miss

Nicholson said, 'When was this, Daisy?'

The maid thought for a moment, and said, 'It would have been while you were both at breakfast yesterday morning. I do hope that I haven't done anything wrong but, you see, the door was open, and –'

'No, you've done nothing wrong, Daisy,' said Gwen. 'Thank you, you may go now.'

The maid left, shutting the door behind her, and Miss Nicholson sat down in the chair opposite Gwen's, saying, 'That settles it then. Violet came in here yesterday and took your key. I'll bet that she saw your clothes on the chair and took those as well.'

'You think that she gave them to Amy, so that she could disguise herself as me?' said Gwen.

'That's exactly what I think,' said Miss Nicholson firmly.

'It's certainly possible,' said Gwen thoughtfully. 'And I have been thinking about my hat, and have realised that it must have been taken when my bedroom was ransacked. I didn't notice that it was missing at the time, for I don't particularly like it and I was thinking of throwing it away.'

'If that is so, then either Amy or Violet – or both of them – are responsible for ransacking your room,' said Miss Nicholson with a grim expression.

'Then there was the time that someone got into my class-room and did all that damage,' said Gwen, looking thoughtful. 'I was convinced that was Amy too, but Daisy was able to clear her name. Oh dear, how horrible it is! I really don't know what to think! Should we tell Miss Grayling of our suspicions?'

'No, for we have no proof,' said Miss Nicholson. 'I think we need to catch the two of them out ourselves.'

'Perhaps you are right,' said Gwen. 'And until we do, we had better make sure that we lock the study door whenever we leave it.'

'I don't think that we should,' said Miss Nicholson. 'We need to make it easy for Amy and Violet to play their tricks so that we can trap them somehow. All the same, we had better be careful what we leave lying around in here. And we must be sure not to let either of the girls think that we suspect them, for that will put them on their guard, you know.'

Violet, meanwhile, quite unaware that she was regarded with such dark suspicion by the two mistresses, was in the Head's study, along with the rest of the first form.

They had already endured a very severe scolding, and Miss Grayling finished off by saying, 'Although midnight feasts are against the rules, I am well aware that most schoolgirls take part in them now and again. But there are other things about this business that concern me greatly.'

She paused to look sternly at the first formers, all of whom were standing with bent heads.

'First of all, you held the feast in a room that was out of bounds,' went on Miss Grayling in a very serious voice. 'A room that you had been put on your honour not to enter. Faith, as head of the form, didn't you feel some sense of responsibility? Didn't it occur to you that you should – at the very least – have stopped the others from using that room?'

Faith bit her lip. It had occurred to her, briefly. But then she had got caught up in the excitement of it all, and had been as thrilled as the others at the thought of having the feast in Miss Lacey's class-room.

'No,' she said honestly, raising her head and looking Miss Grayling in the eye. 'But it should have. I am very sorry, Miss Grayling. We all are.'

'As for you, Violet,' said Miss Grayling. 'What you did was very wrong indeed. You had no right to go into the mistresses' study, never mind stealing Miss Lacey's key.'

The unfortunate Violet trembled like a leaf, and her voice shook as she said, 'I-I didn't think of it as stealing, Miss Grayling. It *wasn't* stealing, for I meant to return it to the study this morning.'

'I daresay,' said Miss Grayling. 'However, I trust that the punishment I give you will make you think twice before you decide to help yourself to someone else's property in the future.'

Miss Grayling looked at the row of bent heads before her, then said, 'You are all confined to school for the next two weeks.'

The first formers groaned inwardly, for this meant no walks on the beach and no trips into town to spend their pocket money. No one protested, though, for they all knew that they had well and truly earned the punishment.

'You, Violet, will apologise to Miss Lacey,' the Head continued, and Violet almost sighed with relief, for she felt that she had got off very lightly. But Miss Grayling hadn't finished.

'You will also go to bed an hour early every night for the next week. And I hope that you will use the time to reflect on what you have done.'

This seemed very harsh indeed to poor Violet. How horrid to have to go to bed when it was still light outside, and the others were in the common-room having fun. But she did not dare argue with the Head, and said meekly, 'Yes, Miss Grayling.'

Daffy, however, had listened to this with a frown and, as she was considerably bolder and more outspoken than Violet, she said, 'But Miss Grayling, didn't Miss Potts tell you that Miss Lacey locked Edith's sister in the shed last night? She doesn't deserve an apology, if you ask me. In fact –'

'I didn't ask you, Daphne,' said Miss Grayling, so coldly that the girl fell silent. 'So kindly keep your opinions to yourself until I ask for them. I have investigated the matter, and the person who locked Lizzie in the shed was most definitely *not* Miss Lacey.'

The first formers looked at one another in astonishment and, unable to hold her tongue, Edith said, 'But it was, Miss Grayling. I beg your pardon, but I saw her with my own eyes.'

'No, Edith,' said the Head. 'The person you saw was someone pretending to be Miss Lacey. Who it was, and what her motive was, I don't know, but I hope that we will get to the bottom of the matter eventually. Now, you may all go to your lesson. Miss Potts knows that you have been with me, so she will excuse you for being late. Edith, not you. I would like a word with you, please.'

As the others trooped out, Edith looked rather alarmed. And her heart sank when Miss Grayling looked at her coldly, and said, 'I find it quite extraordinary, Edith, that you watched someone lock Lizzie in a shed and, rather than letting her out, you simply left her there and went off to enjoy a feast with your friends. Hardly the behaviour of a loyal and loving sister.'

Edith turned red and said, 'I was going to let her out later. You see, Miss Grayling, she found out that we were planning a feast and she meant to sneak. So Lizzie isn't quite as loyal as everyone thinks either.'

'I see,' said the Head, rather shocked at the bitterness in Edith's tone. 'Why do you think that Lizzie intended to sneak?'

'Because she simply can't bear me to have any fun,' Edith burst out. 'She thinks that school is all about studying, and lessons, and exams and –'

'Well, these things are very important,' interrupted the Head.

'I know,' said Edith with a sigh. 'And I do want to do well at those things, Miss Grayling, really I do. But I also want to make friends and enjoy my time at school. But

Lizzie thinks that is wrong. Why, she doesn't even want me to go in for the swimming gala.'

'I see,' said Miss Grayling again, frowning. 'Well, I shall be seeing Lizzie shortly, for no doubt she will come along to report Miss Lacey to me. I will have a talk with her, Edith, and see if I can impress on her the importance of striking a healthy balance between work and play.'

'Thank you, Miss Grayling,' said Edith, though she didn't feel very hopeful. Lizzie had such very firm ideas about things. But if anyone could get through to her, Miss Grayling could.

Unexpected arrivals

'I can't believe that it is almost the last week of term,' said Felicity as she and her friends lazed on the grass one Saturday afternoon after an energetic game of tennis.

'I know, hasn't the time just flown!' said Susan. 'Soon we shall all be packing to go home.'

Never to return to Malory Towers. No one said the words, but they hung, unspoken, in the air, making everyone feel a little melancholy.

None of them wanted to talk about the prospect of not returning to school, so Julie said heartily, 'I'll bet the last two weeks haven't flown by for the first formers. They must be jolly glad that their two-week punishment is up.'

'Silly kids,' said June rather scornfully. 'Having a midnight feast is one thing, but to steal a mistress's key, then hold it in a room which is out of bounds is quite another.'

'That was a strange business,' said Pam. 'We never did find out who it was wandering around that night dressed in Miss Lacey's clothes.'

'I daresay that we never will now,' said Nora. 'A pity, because I hate unsolved mysteries. I always feel . . .'

Suddenly Nora's voice tailed off as she gazed towards the school, and Lucy gave her a nudge, saying, 'You always feel what?'

'I don't know,' said Nora distractedly. 'For I've completely forgotten what I was talking about. I say, Felicity, I've just seen someone go into the school who is the spitting image of your sister Darrell.'

'Darrell?' said Felicity, astonished. 'Oh, that's impossible! What would she be doing at Malory Towers?'

'I don't have the faintest idea,' said Nora. 'But if it wasn't her, it was her double.'

Intrigued, Felicity got to her feet and said, 'I'm going to investigate.'

'I'll come with you,' said Susan. 'It's awfully hot out here, and I need to get into the shade.'

As the two girls walked towards the front door of the school, a voice behind them called out, 'Excuse me, young ladies! I wonder if you might help me?'

Felicity and Susan both turned, to find themselves looking at a tall, distinguished-looking man, with a big moustache and twinkling grey eyes. He doffed his hat in a very gentlemanly manner and said, 'Could you direct me to Miss Grayling's study, please?'

'Of course,' said Felicity politely, wondering who the stranger could be. 'Please come this way.'

The distinguished-looking gentleman proved to be very chatty as he accompanied the girls to Miss Grayling's room.

'I do hope this headmistress of yours isn't a tartar,'

he said jovially, making both of them laugh.

'Not at all,' said Susan. 'She's very pleasant.'

'That's a relief,' said the man. 'For I've come to ask permission to take my two nieces out to tea.'

'Oh, who are your nieces?' asked Felicity. 'I daresay we know them.'

'Lizzie and Edith Mannering,' said the man. 'I meant to come and visit them at half-term, but what with one thing and another I couldn't get away. So I'm hoping that Miss Grayling will take pity on me and allow me to take them out for a treat today.'

'I am quite sure that she will,' said Felicity, trying not to stare at the man. So this was Uncle Charles! And he was very different from the dour, rather grumpy individual that she had pictured.

The two girls left him at Miss Grayling's door, where he thanked them politely, and went on their way. They didn't find anyone resembling Darrell, but, on the landing, Susan paused to look out of the window, and cried, 'My word! Isn't that Irene? And I do believe it's Belinda with her!'

Irene and Belinda had been in Darrell's form, and Felicity rushed to the window to take a look, but she was too late, for the girls Susan had spotted had disappeared from view.

'How odd!' said Felicity. 'First Nora thought that she saw Darrell, and now you have seen Irene and Belinda! What *is* going on?'

The girls found out as they went past the third-form

common-room, and heard a terrific racket coming from inside.

'My goodness!' said Felicity. 'Whatever are those third formers up to in there?'

'Nothing,' said Susan, a puzzled frown on her face. 'Miss Peters has taken them off camping for the rest of the term.'

'So she has!' said Felicity, remembering. 'Then who is in their common-room?'

Just as the girls were wondering if they should investigate, two figures came round the corner.

'Bill and Clarissa!' cried Susan. 'Hallo, you two! Are you here to see Miss Peters? I'm afraid you're out of luck, for she has taken her form camping.'

Bill and Clarissa were two old girls who ran a riding stables near Malory Towers, and they were great friends with the third-form mistress.

'No, we're here for the reunion,' said Bill with a grin.

'What reunion?' said Felicity, puzzled.

'Why, the old girls' reunion, of course,' said Clarissa, pushing open the door of the third-form common-room. 'And here they all are!'

Felicity and Susan stared as if they couldn't believe their eyes! There was Daphne and her little friend Mary-Lou, Irene and Belinda, June's cousin Alicia – and Darrell, with her friend, Sally.

'Felicity!' cried Darrell, coming over to give her sister a hug. 'How marvellous to see you!'

'Well, it's marvellous to see you, too,' said Felicity,

still feeling very surprised indeed. 'You didn't tell me there was going to be a reunion!'

'No, I thought I would surprise you,' laughed Darrell. 'This was all arranged with Miss Grayling at the end of last term. We asked her if we might hold a reunion here, and she said that we could use the third form's common-room and dormitory while they are away on their camping trip.'

'How's that cousin of mine, Felicity?' called out Alicia. 'Still causing trouble?'

'Oh no, June has settled down a great deal since she became games captain, you know.'

'I'm jolly glad to hear it,' said Alicia. 'Now, who's missing? Amanda, Gwen and Mavis.'

'Amanda can't come, for she is at college,' said Sally. 'And Mavis is going to join us later. As for Gwen, well, she is already on the premises, of course, and will be here soon. Miss Grayling has given her a few days off so that she can join our reunion.'

'Super!' said Irene happily. 'My goodness, I feel like a schoolgirl again. I say, wouldn't it be just wizard to have a midnight feast?'

'It's funny you should say that,' said Alicia with a grin. 'I feel just like playing a trick on Mam'zelle Dupont!'

'Yes, but we'd better not discuss such things in front of the Head Girl,' laughed Belinda, waving a hand towards Felicity. 'She might dish out a punishment!'

Felicity and Susan laughed, and Mary-Lou called out, 'Clear off, you kids, and leave us in peace!'

But she was smiling, so Felicity and Susan raised their hands in farewell and wandered off.

'Well!' said Felicity to Susan as they made their way back to their studies. 'The very last thing I expected was to see Darrell and all her friends back here at Malory Towers! That must be what she meant on the first day of term, when she said that she might see me here.'

'I say, let's go outside and give the others the news,' said Susan, slipping her arm through Felicity's. 'Won't June be surprised to learn that Alicia is here?'

Lizzie and Edith, meanwhile, had been startled to be summoned to Miss Grayling's study. They were even more surprised when they entered and saw their Uncle Charles sitting there.

Edith, who had been quite young when she last saw her uncle, was delighted to find that he wasn't nearly as alarming a figure as the one she remembered. As a small girl his booming voice and big moustache had frightened her, but now she simply couldn't understand why, for he seemed a very jolly character.

'Well, girls!' he said, getting to his feet, and enveloping them both in a hug. 'It's very good to see you again. Miss Grayling here has kindly agreed that I may take you out to tea.'

Both girls thanked him politely, then Uncle Charles turned back to Miss Grayling and, picking up his hat, he said, 'I will have them back here by six o'clock at the latest, Miss Grayling. You can rely on me.'

'I'm sure that I can,' said Miss Grayling with a smile. 'Enjoy your outing, girls.'

The sisters did, for Uncle Charles was very entertaining company, and he treated them to a slap-up tea at the little tea-shop in town.

'Super!' said Edith, her eyes shining at the spread that was laid out before them. There were dainty little sandwiches, jam tarts, biscuits and cakes of every kind.

'Tuck in, girls!' urged Uncle Charles, beaming, and the girls did not need to be told twice!

Lizzie was a little reserved with her uncle, but the more outgoing Edith very soon lost her shyness and chattered away to him about all her doings.

'I'm taking part in the swimming gala next week,' she said. 'Oh, Uncle Charles, it would be marvellous if you could come and watch. June – the games captain – thinks that I am certain to win my race. I've been training very hard for diving and swimming, spending every spare minute down at the pool.'

'Edith!' said Lizzie, sharply, shooting her sister a warning glance. Really, what a dreadful chatterbox her young sister was! At this rate, Uncle Charles would think that she spent no time at all studying.

Edith turned red and subsided, but Uncle Charles said, 'I'm jolly pleased to hear that you girls are enjoying yourselves at school. Swimming, eh? Well, I used to be quite a keen swimmer myself as a boy. I will certainly come along if I can. And what about you, Lizzie? What do you enjoy doing in your spare time?'

'Oh, I don't really have much spare time, Uncle Charles,' said Lizzie. 'I'm always busy studying.'

Uncle Charles frowned and said bluntly, 'Well, that can't be good for you! If I'd known that you were going to tire yourself out working all the time, I would never have agreed to pay your school fees.'

Lizzie and Edith looked at one another in consternation, and Lizzie said, 'We do appreciate you lending Mother the money for our fees, Uncle Charles, and –'

'Lending her the money?' said Uncle Charles. 'What nonsense is this? Anyone would think that I expected it to be paid back, and I most certainly don't. I have no children of my own, and I'm only too happy to do what I can for my nieces.'

'But I don't understand,' said Lizzie, looking most perplexed. 'Mother told us that we had to repay you.'

Uncle Charles frowned heavily, then his brow cleared and he gave a guffaw of laughter.

'My dears, your mother has got things quite wrong! I did say that I wanted you both to repay me, but I meant by making the most of your time at Malory Towers – and that means working hard and playing hard. It looks to me, Lizzie, as if you have been doing too much of one and not enough of the other.'

As Lizzie stared at her uncle in astonishment, it was as if a great weight had rolled off her shoulders. Her mother had completely misunderstood Uncle Charles, and because of it she had missed out on an awful lot of fun – and she had given poor Edith a bad time, all for nothing.

Uncle Charles was wagging his finger now, saying, 'I insist that you slack off a bit and have some fun this last week of term. Is that clear?'

Although her uncle's tone was stern, there was a twinkle in his eye, and Lizzie answered it with a broad grin, as she said, 'Perfectly clear, Uncle Charles.'

Edith, looking at her sister, marvelled at the sudden change in her. How much younger and prettier she looked when she smiled. And Edith had a feeling that she would be smiling a lot more from now on!

While the Mannering sisters were having tea with their uncle, Felicity and Susan were strolling along the cliffs when they heard footsteps behind them, and turned to see Darrell walking towards them.

'Hallo there, you two!' she called. 'Felicity, I was hoping to catch you.'

'Would you like to spend some time alone with Felicity?' asked Susan tactfully.

'No, you stay, Susan,' said Darrell. 'For you might be able to help me too. You see, it's about Gwen.'

The two sixth formers looked at Darrell curiously, and she went on, 'Gwen joined our little reunion soon after you two had gone. And it seems to me that something is troubling her. You were right, Felicity, when you wrote to me and said that you thought she had changed. She seems more humble and less boastful, somehow. But when she doesn't realise that anyone is watching her, there is a wistful, rather sad expression on her face.'

'Gwen hasn't had an easy time of it here,' said

Felicity. Then she and Susan went on to explain about the class-room being damaged, and about someone dressing up in her clothes to lock Lizzie in the shed and spoil the first formers' midnight feast.

'There's something else, too,' said Susan. 'I bumped into Daisy, the maid, in the hall a little earlier. You know how she loves a gossip! Somehow she had got to hear about poor Lizzie being locked in the shed, and she was digging for information, though of course I didn't tell her anything!'

'Heavens, is Daisy still here?' said Darrell. 'I remember her starting work at Malory Towers when I was in the fifth form.'

'Yes, but the thing is, Darrell, she told me something jolly interesting,' said Susan. 'Apparently Miss Lacey's room was ransacked a little while ago.'

'I know that,' said Darrell with a frown. 'You've just told me.'

'No, not her class-room – her *bed*room,' said Susan. 'She never reported it to the Head, though.'

'Well, this is certainly a piece of news!' exclaimed Felicity. 'I wonder how Daisy came to hear about it?'

'Oh, the domestic staff seem to hear about everything that goes on at Malory Towers,' said Darrell with a laugh. 'It has always been that way.'

Then her expression grew more serious, and she said, 'It certainly sounds as if someone has it in for poor old Gwen, though. Do you know if she has made any enemies here?'

'Well, a few of the girls aren't too keen on her,' said Felicity. 'But I don't think that any of them would go to those lengths to get back at her.'

'Well, what you have both told me has been very helpful,' said Darrell. 'I wonder if I can encourage Gwen to open up and tell us all of this herself. No doubt she has her own views on who is behind it.'

'I do hope so,' said Susan. Then she glanced at her watch, and said, 'Heavens, just look at the time! We had better turn back, or we'll be late for tea.'

'Are you old girls joining us in the dining-room?' asked Felicity. 'Or are you too grand for us?'

'Oh, we shall be there, all right,' laughed Darrell. 'We will be sitting at the third formers' table while they are away. I must say, I'm looking forward to sitting down and enjoying a Malory Towers tea again!

Reunion at Malory Towers

There was a shock in store for Daffy as she went in to tea that afternoon.

'I say, where is Edith?' she asked the others, as they made their way to the dining-room.

'Oh, her uncle came to visit, and he has taken Edith and her sister out to tea,' said Ivy. 'Lucky Edith! I bet he will have taken them to that little tea-shop in town, where they do those marvellous chocolate cakes.'

'Well, I can't say that I envy her,' said Daffy, pulling a face. 'I wouldn't want to go out to tea with some stern old uncle and a bossy older sister.'

'Yes, Lizzie is rather a wet blanket,' said Katie. 'Though I must say, it's partly Edith's own fault for not standing up to her more.'

'Yes, I gather that Lizzie has always ruled the roost at home,' said Daffy. 'And Edith allowed her to get away with it. My goodness, I would never stand for it if my sister, Sally, spoke to me the way that Lizzie does to Edith. Sally's an awfully good sort, but she would boss me around too, if I let her, for that is what big sisters are like. I showed her right from the start that I wouldn't put up with that sort of nonsense, though. I told her –'

'Daffy!'

Hearing her name called from behind brought Daffy to a halt, and she turned sharply, her mouth dropping open when she saw that the person who had hailed her was none other than Sally.

'S-Sally!' gasped Daffy, staring at her sister as if she couldn't believe her eyes. 'What on earth are you doing here?'

'Why, I am here for the old girls' reunion,' said Sally, ruffling her sister's curly hair. 'Mother was going to write and tell you that I was coming, but I thought it would be a nice surprise if I just turned up unexpectedly.'

'Well, it's certainly a surprise,' said Daffy, who didn't quite know whether to feel dismayed or delighted.

She was terribly fond of her big sister, of course, but she certainly didn't want Sally keeping a watchful eye on her!

'Goodness me, Daffy!' said Sally, eyeing Daffy critically. 'Whatever have you been doing, with one sock up and one sock down? Do tidy yourself up!'

Hastily, Daffy bent over and pulled up the offending sock. Then, to the amusement of the watching first formers, Sally straightened the girl's tie, before standing back and saying, 'There, that looks much neater. Off you go now, or you will be late for tea, and that will never do!'

'Yes, Sally,' said Daffy meekly, her cheeks turning pink as she saw the others struggling to control their mirth.

Sally strode past the first formers and went to join

the others, who were already seated at the third formers' table.

Mam'zelle Dupont, quite overcome with delight at seeing so many of her old favourites again, was standing by Darrell's chair, her hand on the girl's shoulder and a beam of pleasure on her face.

'Ah, how good it is to see you again – and what fine young ladies you have all grown into!' she cried. 'But where is Mavis?'

'She will be along later,' said Irene. 'Of course, Mam'zelle, you know that our Mavis is now a great opera singer, don't you?'

'Yes, indeed,' said Mam'zelle. 'The dear girl sent me one of her records, and what pleasure it gives me to listen to her voice.'

'I bet that Mavis has gone all high-and-mighty boastful again now that she is famous,' murmured Alicia to Darrell and Sally.

'Well, if she has, we shall soon bring her back down to earth with a good dose of Malory Towers common sense!' said Sally firmly.

'I say, who is that young woman over at the mistresses' table?' asked Mary-Lou. 'She must be new.'

'Yes, she looks rather jolly,' said Belinda.

'Oh, that's Miss Nicholson,' said Gwen, helping herself to a slice of bread and butter. 'She is the Geography mistress, and a very good sort. She and I are the best of friends.'

The others looked at one another in surprise, for

the plain, sensible-looking Miss Nicholson was the very last person they would have expected Gwen to be friends with.

'Heavens!' whispered Daphne to Mary-Lou. 'Gwen really *has* changed!'

As it was such a warm and pleasant evening, many of the girls went for a stroll in the grounds after tea.

Darrell and her friends picked a sunny spot on the lawn near the big driveway and sat down.

'Your friend, Miss Nicholson, will be missing your company while you are with us at the reunion,' remarked Sally.

'Yes, though she quite understood that I couldn't pass up the opportunity to join in the reunion,' said Gwen.

'You must introduce us to her,' said Darrell, thinking that she might be able to get some information from Miss Nicholson. 'Perhaps she would like to join us in the common-room tonight? I am sure it will be much more pleasant for her than sitting alone in her study.'

'Oh, thank you,' said Gwen, flushing with pleasure. 'I will ask her, for I'm sure that she will enjoy the company.'

'Here, look what's coming up the drive!' cried Daphne suddenly. 'My word, did you ever see a car that size before?'

The sixth formers turned their heads, and saw a very long, very expensive-looking car making its way up the drive.

'Goodness!' said Mary-Lou, her eyes almost starting

from her head. 'Who on earth can this be?'

A group of sixth formers were standing nearby and they, too, wondered who the occupant could be.

At last, the car drew to a halt, and a uniformed chauffeur got out, opening one of the back doors.

The young woman who emerged drew gasps of admiration from the watching girls, for she was slim, elegant and *very* expensively dressed. Her red hair was piled up on top of her head, while diamonds glittered in her ears and at her throat.

'I know who that is!' cried Amy. 'It's Mavis Allyson, the opera singer. My parents took me to hear her sing in Rome during the holidays and she was simply stunning. Oh, I wonder if she would give me her autograph?'

Of course, Amy wasn't the only one to have recognised Mavis, and scores of eyes followed her progress as she daintily approached the old girls. Several younger girls would have liked to ask for an autograph, but Mavis looked so haughty and unapproachable that no one dared!

'Just as I thought,' whispered Alicia to the others. 'Fame has gone to Mavis's head.'

'Oh, what a shame!' replied Darrell in dismay. 'When she left Malory Towers she had really settled down and become one of us.'

'Well, she needn't think that she's going to queen it over us!' said Irene indignantly. 'Mavis isn't going to spoil our reunion.'

Mavis was almost upon them now, and she looked so

grand that, instinctively, Mary-Lou made to get up. But Daphne pulled her back down again, saying, 'She's not royalty, Mary-Lou – even though she might think she is.'

'How lovely to see you all,' said Mavis, in a bored, rather affected voice. 'Of course, I am dreadfully busy these days, but I managed to make time to fit the reunion in.'

'We're honoured,' said Alicia bitingly.

'I should jolly well think you are!' said Mavis. 'Don't you know that I'm an opera singer now?'

Then her face split into a broad grin, and – to the astonishment of the others – she threw her head back, roaring with laughter.

'Oh, your faces!' she cried when she had stopped laughing. 'I knew that you would be wondering if I had gone back to my old, unpleasant ways, so I thought I'd play a little trick on you!'

'You wretch, Mavis!' cried Darrell, also laughing.

'Yes, I must admit, one or two of us did wonder if fame would have changed you,' said Alicia, having the grace to blush a little. 'Do sit down – or don't you want to get that expensive-looking dress of yours dirty?'

'As if I care for that!' said Mavis, flopping down on to the grass beside Alicia. 'I say, isn't it marvellous to be together again?'

'Do you always travel by chauffeur-driven car, Mavis?' asked Daphne curiously.

'Of course not!' laughed Mavis. 'I persuaded the director of my opera company to lend me his car and chauffeur for the day, just so that I could make a grand entrance.'

'Well, you certainly had us fooled,' laughed Belinda.

'It's ten minutes to six,' said Sally, looking at her watch. 'You know that Miss Grayling asked us all to go to her study at six.'

'So she did,' said Darrell. 'Oh, won't it be wonderful to see her again?'

'I feel rather nervous about it,' said Mary-Lou with a little laugh.

'Nonsense, why should you?' said Alicia, giving her a little push. 'Just remember that you are a nursing sister now, Mary-Lou, not a schoolgirl. I'm sure that when you are at work you must be reliable, responsible and confident, or they wouldn't let you loose on the wards!'

'I am,' said Mary-Lou. 'It's funny, though, now that I am back at Malory Towers I feel like a timid little schoolgirl again!'

As it turned out, Mary-Lou wasn't the only one who felt as if she had gone back in time when faced with Miss Grayling.

There were some people, thought Darrell, as the old girls sat in the Head's study, who naturally commanded respect. And, unquestionably, Miss Grayling was one of them.

But the Head very soon put the girls at their ease, asking each of them in turn what paths their lives had followed. Irene, of course, had pursued a career in music, while Belinda was making a name as an artist. Daphne was working as a secretary in her father's office. Sally had just started teaching at an infants school and was loving every minute of it. As for the clever, quick-witted Alicia, she had found a career where she could put her brains to good use, and had surprised everyone by joining the police force!

'Well!' Darrell had exclaimed on hearing this piece of news. 'That's certainly something you can get your teeth into. It would take a jolly cunning criminal to outwit you, Alicia.'

'Gwen, I need not ask what you are doing, of course,' said the Head, with a smile. 'Or you, Bill and Clarissa. I am glad that you have managed to leave the stables for a few days to come and join us.'

'Two of my brothers are looking after things while we are here,' said Bill. 'We wouldn't have missed this reunion for the world.'

'Well, at least you can relax and enjoy yourselves, knowing that your horses are in good hands,' said Miss Grayling. Then she turned to Mavis, saying, with a smile, 'I imagine that everyone in the country must know your name by now. And Darrell, Felicity tells me that you are a reporter on a newspaper.'

'Yes, Miss Grayling,' said Darrell with a smile. 'I enjoy it tremendously, for I've always loved writing. In fact . . .'

She paused, for she had received a piece of very good news the day before. But perhaps mentioning it here, in front of the others, would seem like boasting.

Sally, who already knew what the news was, spoke

up, saying, 'Go on, Darrell. Tell everyone!'

The girls and Miss Grayling were all looking very curious now, and, clearing her throat, Darrell said, 'I have been writing a children's book in my spare time, and a little while ago I sent it off to a publisher. It was just a spur of the moment decision, and I never dreamed that anyone would be interested in it, but – well, they have decided to publish it.'

'My dear, that is marvellous news!' exclaimed Miss Grayling.

And the girls agreed, all gathering round Darrell to clap her on the back and offer their congratulations.

'Good for you, Darrell!'

'Just think, when you are a famous author we will be able to say that we were at school with you!'

'If anyone deserves success it's you, Darrell!'

'What is your book about?' asked Gwen.

Darrell laughed, a little self-consciously, and said, 'Well, actually it's about a girls' boarding school – not unlike Malory Towers.'

Everyone was simply thrilled to hear this, and Miss Grayling said with a smile, 'You will certainly have been able to draw on your personal experience for that, Darrell.'

The conversation continued for several more minutes, then the Head said, 'It is very good to have you all back here as responsible adults, even if it is only for a few days. I hope that you will have a pleasant reunion, and that it brings back many happy memories for you.'

'Well, we are very grateful to you for having us,' said Darrell.

The old girls made their way back to the common-room in a dignified manner, then, as soon as the door had closed behind them, Irene jumped in the air and cried, 'Hurrah, we're back at Malory Towers!'

Alicia grinned and shook her head. 'Honestly, Irene, I don't think that you will *ever* grow up and be a responsible adult!'

A shock for Gwen

Lizzie and Edith were delivered back to Malory Towers at six o'clock precisely, as their uncle had promised. Before the girls got out of the car, Uncle Charles took his wallet from his pocket and removed two notes, handing one to each girl.

Both of them gasped, and Lizzie said, 'Uncle Charles! We can't possibly accept this. Why, it's almost the end of term and we will never manage to spend this amount.'

'Well, if you have any left over you can spend it in the holidays,' said Uncle Charles firmly. 'I must have a word with your mother and see about making you both a proper allowance next term. And Edith, it looks as if you need a new uniform as well. Make sure that your mother gets you one, and tell her to send the bill to me.'

'Oh, but you've already been so generous!' said Edith. 'I couldn't let you –'

'Now, that's quite enough!' interrupted her uncle with mock sternness. 'My word, I've never known such argumentative girls, and very disrespectful it is too! All that you have to do, my dears, is say, "Thank you, Uncle Charles," and that is an end to the matter.'

The two sisters exchanged glances and smiled, then,

obediently, they chorused, 'Thank you, Uncle Charles!'

The two of them were chattering nineteen to the dozen as they entered the big hall, and Lizzie, spotting Alice, hailed her.

'Hallo!' said Alice. 'You two look as if you have had a wonderful time.'

'Oh, we have,' said Lizzie, her eyes sparkling as she put her arm through Alice's. 'Do come to my study and I will tell you all about it. Edith, off you go and have fun with your friends. I will see you tomorrow.'

Alice stared at Lizzie in astonishment. Why, she had never seen the girl look so relaxed and happy before! There was a kind of glow about her that made her look really pretty. And were Alice's ears deceiving her, or had Lizzie actually told her young sister to go off and have fun?

'Come along, then,' she said to Lizzie. 'I am simply dying to hear what you have been up to!'

In the third-form common-room, the old girls had been joined by Miss Nicholson, who had been delighted when Gwen told her that her friends wanted to meet her. She was about the same age as the others, and they soon warmed to her friendly, open personality.

'Gwen, I hope that we are going to see this marvellous class-room of yours,' said Darrell. 'Felicity tells me that it's quite magnificent.'

'Well, I don't know that I would go that far,' said Gwen. 'But it's certainly a little different from the other class-rooms in the school.'

'Will you be returning next term?' asked Sally curiously.

'I don't know yet,' answered Gwen. 'This term was a sort of experiment, to see how I fitted in and how the classes went. I shall have to wait and see what Miss Grayling thinks.'

She spoke airily, but, inside, she was very worried indeed that the Head might not want her to come back next term. The classes had gone well, on the whole – better than Gwen had expected, in fact. But she seemed to have been at the centre of rather a lot of trouble, even though none of it was her fault. Perhaps Miss Grayling might think that she was more trouble than she was worth!

'Well, I think you've done marvellously,' declared Miss Nicholson. 'Especially when one considers all the setbacks . . .'

But Gwen flashed her friend a warning glance. The others were doing so well in their chosen careers, and she still had enough pride not to want them to know of her problems.

Hastily, she said, 'I shall show you all the class-room tomorrow morning. I do hope that you will like it.'

Just then, there was a tap at the door, and Daisy entered.

'Excuse me, young ladies,' she said. 'The housekeeper wanted me to tell you that there are extra blankets in the big cupboard just outside your dormitory, just in case any of you should get chilly during the night.'

'Thank you, Daisy,' said Clarissa. 'It's quite warm though, so I am sure we will be fine.'

'Will you be sleeping in the dormitory too, Miss Lacey?' asked the maid. 'Or are you going back to your own room?'

'Oh, I shall be sleeping in the dorm, all right,' said Gwen. 'I should feel quite left out if I had to go to my own room.'

'What a pity we don't have an extra bed,' said Belinda to Miss Nicholson. 'Or you could have joined us too.'

Alicia was just about to ask Miss Nicholson how she liked it at Malory Towers, when she became aware that Daisy was still hovering, and said, 'Thanks, Daisy. You can go now.'

'Well, if you're sure there is nothing that you need,' said Daisy, seeming rather reluctant to leave. But, as Alicia had told her to go, she really had no choice.

'You were rather sharp with old Daisy, weren't you?' said Bill, once the door had shut.

Alicia shrugged, and said, 'I never liked her, even when we were pupils here. She's a great deal too nosy for my liking.'

'Oh, she's not a bad sort,' said Gwen.

Alicia laughed. 'You've certainly changed your opinion of her! I remember how spiteful you were to her when she first started here as a maid.'

'Me?' said Gwen, quite astonished. 'Oh, Alicia, I wasn't!'

'You were, Gwen,' said Mary-Lou. 'I remember it

well. You were always getting poor Daisy to run errands for you, and you would give her the most tremendous scolds if she made the slightest mistake.'

'Yes, you made the poor girl's life a misery, until Darrell stepped in and ticked you off,' said Belinda.

'Oh!' cried Gwen, pressing her hands to her hot cheeks as the memories flooded back. 'I had quite forgotten that! What a mean little beast I was!'

'Well, it seems that Daisy has forgotten it too,' said Miss Nicholson. 'Thank heavens she doesn't bear you any grudge.'

Just then Mavis put her hand over her mouth to stifle a yawn. 'Gosh, I'm tired after that long drive,' she said. 'If no one minds, I think I might turn in soon.'

She removed her diamond necklace and earrings as she spoke, dropping them into her handbag, and Daphne said, 'Mavis, you really ought to give your jewellery to Matron, to put in her safe. It looks awfully expensive.'

'It does, doesn't it?' laughed Mavis. 'But they are not real diamonds, you know. This is just cheap costume jewellery that I bought so that I could look the part of the great opera singer when I turned up here!'

The others laughed too, then Mavis, along with Daphne and Mary-Lou, who had also had long journeys, went off to the dormitory.

Presently, Miss Nicholson left too, and Darrell stared after her thoughtfully. She had seen the warning look Gwen had given her friend when she had mentioned something about setbacks. Perhaps, she thought, it might be helpful to talk to Miss Nicholson alone, and see what she could get out of her.

As things turned out, though, Darrell didn't need to speak to Miss Nicholson!

'Anyone fancy a swim after breakfast?' asked Lizzie over breakfast on Sunday morning.

The sixth formers looked up from their meal in surprise. It wasn't like Lizzie to suggest anything like that!

'Um – yes, I wouldn't mind,' said Felicity, feeling that the girl ought to be encouraged. 'What about you, Susan?'

'Yes, why not?' said her friend. 'It's far too nice a day to stay indoors.'

One or two others said that they would also enjoy a swim, while Alice, who wasn't fond of the water, said that she would come along and watch.

'Whatever has got into Lizzie?' Felicity asked Alice as the sixth formers walked down to the pool a little later. 'I've never known her be so friendly and jolly. Is this your doing?'

'I'd like to take the credit,' said Alice with a smile. 'But you must thank her uncle.'

And, quickly, Alice told Felicity the tale that Lizzie had related to her last night.

'Well!' exclaimed Felicity, at the end. 'So Lizzie got the wrong end of the stick. Or rather, her mother did. Thank goodness Lizzie has decided to slacken off a bit and enjoy the rest of the term.'

'Yes, and it will make life easier for young Edith, too,' said Alice. 'I think both of them are going to find their next term a lot more enjoyable.'

'Oh, don't talk about next term!' wailed Felicity. 'For we shan't be here, and sometimes it makes me feel so sad!'

'Then you must make the most of the little time you have left,' said Alice sensibly.

'Yes, that's exactly what Darrell said to me,' said Felicity. 'She was quite right, and so are you. Last one in the pool is a rotten egg!'

The sixth formers had a marvellous time, and no one enjoyed herself more than Lizzie.

'Why, you're almost as good a swimmer as your young sister!' exclaimed June, after narrowly beating the girl in a race. 'Fancy keeping that to yourself! If only I had known, you could have had a place in the gala too!'

'That's why I didn't let you know,' said Lizzie with a self-conscious little laugh. 'I was afraid that you might expect me to practise swimming when I wanted to study.' Lizzie paused for a moment, then went on, 'Look, June, I've been an idiot this term, trying to persuade you to drop Edith from the gala. I'm just glad now that you didn't take any notice of me. And I'm sorry.'

June had never cared much for Lizzie, but she admired her now for being able to own up to a fault. She clapped the girl on the back, saying, 'There's no need to apologise, for I see that you were doing what you thought was right. I'm just glad you have come to realise there is more to school than books. How about a race back to the other end of the pool?'

'You're on!' said Lizzie at once, her eyes dancing.

This was the scene that greeted the old girls as they walked down the cliff path to the pool.

'Gosh, Alicia, just look at your cousin June go!' cried Bill. 'She's awfully fast.'

'Yes, that other girl isn't far behind her, though,' said Alicia, watching critically.

'What luck that the swimming gala is taking place on Wednesday,' said Sally. 'I shall be able to cheer on young Daffy, and Darrell and Alicia can support Felicity and June.'

'I say, who is that seated at the side, watching?' asked Mary-Lou. 'I can't quite place her.'

'Why, that must be Jo Jones – or Alice, as she is known now,' said Darrell.

Almost as though she knew someone was talking about her, Alice turned her head. She got politely to her feet as the old girls approached, feeling rather apprehensive. The last time she had seen any of them was when she had been in the second form, and her behaviour then had left a lot to be desired. But, thanks to the sixth formers, Darrell and the others knew that Alice had changed, and all of them were prepared to let bygones be bygones. They greeted her in a friendly manner, and stood chatting to her until Daphne said, 'Mavis, that girl is at the top of the cliff path. The one who was waiting for you when you came out of the dormitory.'

'Oh, she wanted an autograph,' said Mavis with a laugh. 'Which I was quite happy to give her, of course.'

'Why, that's Amy, from our form,' said Alice, shielding her eyes from the sun as she looked at the figure standing at the top of the cliff path. 'I wonder what she is doing here, for she's not a great one for outdoor life!'

In fact, Amy was suffering from a bad dose of hero worship, and was following Mavis around in much the same way that Violet had been following her all term!

The girl had been up and dressed at a very early hour, and had waited outside the third-form dormitory for Mavis to come out, so that she might get her autograph. Mavis had been very chatty and friendly and, remembering how grand and aloof she had seemed when she arrived, Amy assumed that the young opera singer had taken a liking to her.

Now an idea had come into her head. Her mother was giving a grand summer party in the holidays. How marvellous it would be if she, Amy, could persuade Mavis to be the guest of honour, and perhaps sing at the party. Her mother would be delighted, of course. Amy could almost hear her saying, 'Well, of course, Miss Allyson is a great friend of my daughter's, you know, and she agreed to sing at my party as a favour to her.'

Goodness, wouldn't that make everyone sit up and take notice!

So, as the old girls reached the top of the cliff path,

on their way to Miss Lacey's class-room, Amy was lying in wait.

'Oh, Miss Allyson,' she breathed. 'I wonder if I might have a word?'

But Mavis's attention was being claimed by Daphne, and she didn't even hear Amy.

The sixth former trotted along patiently behind the old girls, until they were almost back at North Tower, then at last her chance came, and she said, 'Miss Allyson!'

Mavis turned, and said, 'Why, hallo again, Amy. Don't tell me that you want another autograph?'

'Oh, no,' said Amy. 'I just wanted to ask –'

'Hurry up, Mavis!' called out Alicia. 'We have to go and say hello to all the mistresses, and Gwen is simply itching to show us her class-room.'

'I'm coming!' called Mavis. Then she turned back to Amy, patting her on the arm and saying, 'Excuse me, Amy, but I really must go. Perhaps we will have the chance to talk later.'

As Amy stood gazing worshipfully after Mavis, she, too, was being watched. Violet and Faith, sitting on a bench nearby, had witnessed the whole thing.

'Well!' laughed Faith. 'It looks as though Mavis has got herself an admirer.'

Violet, who had been quite horrified by the little scene, said nothing. She had set Amy up on a pedestal, and to see her trotting after someone else with an adoring expression on her face just didn't seem right somehow.

'Now you see how silly *you* look,' said Faith unkindly.

'What nonsense!' said Violet sharply. 'I don't talk in that silly, breathless voice, and make my eyes as big as saucers when I am with Amy.'

'Oh yes, you do, my girl,' said Faith with a grin.

'Do I really?' asked Violet, shocked.

Faith nodded, and, quite suddenly, Violet *did* see how silly she had been. And, just as suddenly, her admiration for Amy completely disappeared, as though it had never existed. Amy wasn't some marvellous, extraordinary person, she was just an ordinary schoolgirl with rather a high opinion of herself. And, by hanging around after Mavis, she had fallen off her pedestal, and Violet had seen her quite clearly.

The old girls, meanwhile, were having a marvellous time. They had already spoken to Mam'zelle Dupont, of course, and now they went to visit Mam'zelle Rougier, Miss Potts, Miss Linnie, the art mistress – and last, but not least, Matron.

'Well, well, well!' said Matron, beaming at them. 'How grown-up you all look. It's nice to be able to welcome you back here without having to warn you against having midnight feasts, or asking for your health certificates!'

'Matron, have you been dyeing your hair?' asked Alicia cheekily. 'I'm sure you had more grey hairs last time I saw you.'

'The grey has slowed down a little since you left, Alicia,' retorted Matron. 'Although that cousin of yours has done her best to take over where you left off. Thank heavens she's settled down a bit now that she is in the sixth form!'

Then, of course, the girls had to see Gwen's classroom. Gwen unlocked the door, and stood back for the others to go in before her.

They exclaimed over the furnishings and ornaments, then Clarissa said, 'It looks as if you have forgotten to clean the blackboard after your last lesson.'

'Oh no, that's impossible, for Bonnie cleaned it for me.'

'Well, there's certainly something written here now,' said Sally, going up to the blackboard. Then she turned pale, and, as the others gathered round and read what was written there, a shocked silence fell.

The words were chalked in big, capital letters, and said:

'HALLO, OLD GIRLS. I'M SURE THAT MISS LACEY DOESN'T WANT TO SPOIL YOUR REUNION BY TELLING YOU WHY SHE WAS DISMISSED FROM HER LAST POSITION, SO I WILL. MISS LACEY IS A COMMON THIEF.'

A very successful gala

The silence was suddenly broken by the sound of sobbing, and everyone turned, horrified to see that Gwen had burst into noisy tears.

Darrell took charge at once, leading Gwen to a sofa.

'I'm not a thief,' Gwen sobbed piteously. 'I'm not.'

'Of course you're not,' said Mary-Lou, who always hated to see anyone upset. 'We know that, and I can't think why someone would write such a thing.'

Some of the others, however, weren't so sure, and they exchanged glances. Gwen had played some mean tricks during her time as a pupil at the school, and her nature had been a sly and spiteful one. Perhaps she hadn't changed so much after all.

'Gwen, dear,' said Darrell, sitting down beside the young woman and taking her hand. 'You must tell us what this is all about. I may as well tell you, I know that someone has been playing horrid tricks on you since you came back to Malory Towers. Is this another of them?'

Gwen produced a dainty handkerchief from her bag and blew her nose, before looking round at the watching girls.

'Yes, it is,' she said. 'But it's true. I was dismissed from my last post for stealing.'

A gasp went round, and Gwen said defiantly, 'But I was falsely accused, and stole nothing.'

'What happened, Gwen?' asked Sally. 'It might help if you tell us.'

'Very well,' said Gwen, giving a sniff. 'But would one of you fetch Miss Nicholson, please? She has been a true friend to me, and I would like her to hear this too.'

'I'll go,' said Mary-Lou at once, dashing from the room.

There was an awkward silence while the others waited for Mary-Lou to return with Miss Nicholson. Fortunately, as it was Sunday, she had no classes to teach, and Mary-Lou soon found her in her study, where she told her what had happened.

Gwen had composed herself a little by the time they returned and, once everyone had seated themselves on the chairs and sofas, she began, 'After I left finishing school, I took a job as companion to an elderly widow, Mrs Carruthers. She was a friend of Mother's, you see, and I thought that she would treat me as one of the family.'

'But she didn't?' prompted Alicia as Gwen's eyes began to fill up again.

'No, she made it clear that she thought she was doing me a great favour by giving me the job,' said Gwen. 'She even hinted that she was doing Mother a favour by not ending their friendship once Father was taken ill, and we were no longer wealthy.'

'What a horrible woman!' cried Miss Nicholson.

'Yes, she was horrible,' said Gwen, managing a little smile. 'She treated me like dirt, expecting me to be at her beck and call at all hours. Then one day a valuable antique vase went missing from her drawing-room, and I was accused.'

'But why did she think it was you, Gwen?' asked Mavis.

'Because the cook and the maids had worked for Mrs Carruthers for years,' said Gwen. 'And nothing had ever gone missing before. Besides, she knew that my family had fallen on hard times, so I suppose she thought that gave me a motive.'

'And she dismissed you?' said Sally.

Gwen nodded, and said bitterly, 'She searched my bedroom first, but even though the vase wasn't there, Mrs Carruthers refused to believe in my innocence. I was sent packing, without a reference or the wages that she owed me, and was told that I was lucky the police hadn't been called.'

'Well!' said Irene, shocked. 'I wonder who did steal the vase, then?'

'That's just it,' said Gwen. 'No one did. Miss Winter, my old governess, bumped into Mrs Carruthers' cook about a month after I had been dismissed. It turned out that one of the maids had broken the vase and been afraid to own up to it straight away. She was away visiting her family when I was accused, but when she came back and heard what had happened she was awfully upset, and admitted breaking the vase at once.'

'I see,' said Belinda. 'And did Mrs Carruthers offer you your job back?'

Gwen shook her head. 'No, not that I would have accepted the offer. She didn't contact me at all, or apologise, or send me the wages I was owed. In fact, if Miss Winter hadn't bumped into the cook that day, I would never have known that my name had been cleared.'

'Well, it sounds to me as if you are well out of it,' said Darrell. 'Gwen, does Miss Grayling know about this?'

'Yes,' said Gwen. 'I had to explain why I didn't have a reference, you see. And I wanted to be honest about it from the start. But I asked her not to tell anyone else, for I know that there are always some people who will say that there is no smoke without fire.'

'I am quite sure none of us think that,' said Miss Nicholson, looking round the room.

Everyone agreed at once, for even those who had doubted Gwen believed her now.

'The question is, who wrote that message on the blackboard?' said Miss Nicholson. 'For whoever it is must be the person who has played those other beastly tricks on you.'

'What other tricks?' asked Daphne, her eyes wide.

Aided by Miss Nicholson, Gwen told the others of the things that had happened to her.

'We think that Amy of the sixth form might be responsible, for it's no secret that she dislikes me intensely,' finished Gwen.

The girls were very shocked, of course, and there were a great many exclamations of disgust. One person who said nothing, however, was Alicia, who sat gazing thoughtfully into space. As Alicia was someone who usually had plenty to say for herself, Darrell asked, 'What are you thinking, Alicia?'

'I'm thinking that perhaps Amy isn't the culprit,' said Alicia, frowning. 'There's another person whose name seems to come into this rather a lot – Daisy. She took Gwen's clothes to be cleaned, and it was her word that proved Amy wasn't responsible for damaging the flower arrangement.'

'Well, one thing is for certain,' said Bill. 'Whoever wrote that message on the blackboard had a key to this room. And I would imagine that it would be an easy matter for Daisy to get hold of the key.'

'Yes, but it would be quite an easy matter for anyone to get hold of it,' pointed out Miss Nicholson. 'The housekeeper has the key on a hook in her room, it would only take an instant to slip in and get it while she wasn't there.'

'Yes, but how could Daisy – or anyone else, for that matter – have known about Gwen being dismissed from her last position?' asked Belinda.

'I never thought of that,' said Gwen, looking puzzled. 'I can't imagine . . . yes, I can, though! Shortly after I arrived here I had a letter from my mother, and it went missing. Mother mentioned Mrs Carruthers and the whole incident in the letter. That was why I was so concerned when it disappeared, for I was worried that it would fall into the wrong hands.'

'And it seems that it did,' said Miss Nicholson gravely.

'Susan told me yesterday that Daisy was trying to get information out of her,' said Darrell, rubbing her nose. 'She was talking about the time Lizzie was locked in the shed, and the time someone got into Gwen's bedroom . . .'

'But Daisy didn't know about that,' Miss Nicholson interrupted. 'No one did, apart from Gwen and me, for she didn't report it.'

'Then the only way Daisy could have known about it is if she was the culprit,' said Darrell heavily. 'That settles it.'

'It seems that I was wrong,' said Miss Nicholson, looking upset. 'Daisy *has* been holding a grudge.'

'And she has slipped up by telling Susan about the bedroom incident,' said Belinda. 'Well, if she has slipped up once, she can slip up again.'

'Yes, but we can't leave it to chance, with only a few days to go until the end of term,' said Alicia. 'Daisy must be *made* to slip up.'

'But how, Alicia?' asked Sally.

'I think those very valuable diamonds of Mavis's might provide the answer,' said Alicia.

'But they're not valuable, Alicia,' said Mavis, puzzled. 'I told you, they are just paste.'

'My dear Mavis,' said Alicia, going across and laying a

hand on the girl's shoulder, 'you are quite mistaken. That jewellery is very valuable indeed – worth a fortune, in fact. And we are going to use it to bait a trap for Daisy.'

'I think I see what you are getting at,' said Mary-Lou excitedly. 'We know that Daisy has stolen once, for she took the cufflinks that Gwen had bought for her father. And if she has stolen once, she may do so again.'

'Especially if temptation is put in her way,' said Alicia with a grin.

The last week of term was a very busy one. There were desks and cupboards to clear out, trunks to be packed, and – of course – the swimming gala to look forward to. June was very wrapped up in the organisation, for it would be her last duty as games captain, and she was determined that it should go smoothly. Felicity and Susan, as well as taking part, were helping her, but June always seemed to find something to worry about.

'What if more parents than we expect turn up?'

'What if no one turns up at all?'

'Felicity, have you had the programmes printed yet?'

'Susan, can you check that the life-belt has come back from being mended?'

'Do stop fretting,' said the placid Pam. 'I'm quite sure that everything will go – er – swimmingly.'

Everyone groaned at this but, as June had feared, things did not go quite as swimmingly as she had hoped!

'Disaster has struck!' she cried, bursting into Felicity's study on the day before the gala.

'Heavens!' said Felicity, who had been enjoying a chat with Susan. 'What on earth has happened, June?'

'Cathy of the fifth form has gone down with chicken pox and been sent home,' said June, sinking down into a chair and burying her face in her hands. 'And she was taking part in the senior backstroke race tomorrow.'

'Call on one of the reserves,' said Susan sensibly.

'They have both gone down with chicken pox too,' said June glumly. 'There seems to have been an outbreak in the fifth form. Oh, what am I to do?'

While the others considered this, someone knocked on the door, and Lizzie came in, saying in a breezy manner, 'Has anyone seen Alice? We were supposed to be going for a walk together.'

No one had, but a light came into June's eyes as they rested on Lizzie, and she leaped up with a cry that made the others jump.

'Never mind going for a walk, my girl,' said June, taking Lizzie by the shoulders. 'You are going to get some swimming practice in, for you're taking part in the gala tomorrow.'

'Am I?' said Lizzie, startled.

'You are,' said June firmly. 'And you need to practise your backstroke. Any objections?'

'None at all,' said Lizzie. 'My uncle may be coming to watch, and it will be nice for him to have both nieces taking part.'

'I simply can't get over the change in Lizzie,' laughed Felicity, when June had led Lizzie off to the pool.

'What a pity that her uncle didn't turn up earlier in the term!'

There was a surprise in store for the Mannering sisters on the day of the gala, for not only did Uncle Charles turn up, but he brought their mother with him!

'Mother!' cried both girls, flinging their arms around her. 'What a wonderful surprise!'

'Well, when your uncle telephoned and offered to drive me to the school, I simply couldn't resist,' said Mrs Mannering, a pretty woman, who looked very like her daughters. 'I thought that it would make up for missing half-term. Edith, darling, I am simply dying to watch you swim.'

'Oh, it's not just me that you will be watching,' laughed Edith. 'Lizzie is in one of the races as well.'

'Oh, that's marvellous!' cried Mrs Mannering, looking hard at her older daughter and feeling pleased that she had lost her rather serious expression, and now seemed like a happy, carefree schoolgirl. She blamed herself for the strain that Lizzie had placed herself under, and now, as she put an arm about each girl's shoulder, she said, 'My dears, I can't tell you how sorry I am for misunderstanding what Uncle Charles said to me. I can't believe that I was foolish enough to think that such a generous man would really expect us to repay him for your school fees.'

'Now, that's quite enough of that!' said Uncle Charles, turning a little red. 'This is supposed to be a happy occasion for us.'

'Yes,' said Lizzie, squeezing her mother's hand. 'It was just a mistake, Mother, so let's forget all about it.'

In the end, despite June's misgivings, the gala went off very well indeed. Mrs Mannering had the thrill of seeing Edith receive a standing ovation for her graceful diving, while Lizzie finished a very honourable second in her race.

Neither Felicity's parents nor June's had been able to come, but Darrell applauded wildly at Felicity's impressive diving, while Alicia yelled herself hoarse as June streaked the length of the swimming pool, narrowly beating her opponents. Sally was there to spur Daffy on, too, of course, her heart in her mouth as she watched the girl poised on the topmost diving board. How tiny she looked, all the way up there! Sally squeezed Darrell's hand involuntarily as Daffy launched herself into the air, turning a perfect somersault, before stretching out her arms and legs and diving cleanly into the water.

'That was simply marvellous!' said Alicia, clapping June on the back when everyone went in to tea afterwards. 'To think that my don't-careish cousin was responsible for organising all that!'

'I'm not *quite* so don't-careish now, if you don't mind, Alicia,' said June with a grin. 'But I mustn't take all the credit, for Felicity and Susan were an enormous help to me.'

'You were excellent too,' said Darrell to Felicity. 'I was proud of you. And I managed to get some decent photographs, so Mother and Daddy will be able to share your moment of glory as well.'

All of the Malory Towers girls went to bed without protesting that night, tired but happy. Only the old girls – along with Miss Nicholson – sat up late.

'Well, today has been fun,' said Clarissa. 'But tomorrow is not going to be fun at all.'

'I just hope that everything goes according to plan,' said Mavis, looking worried.

'As long as everyone plays their parts, nothing can go wrong,' said Alicia, confidently. 'Everything will be all right, you'll see.'

'Oh, I do hope so,' said Gwen, wringing her hands. 'Miss Grayling hasn't said anything yet about me coming back next term. If she does, I would very much like to accept her offer, but I don't feel that I can if Daisy is still here, planning and plotting against me.'

'She won't be,' said Darrell, a grim expression on her face. 'Dear Daisy is in for a shock tomorrow!'

20

Goodbye Malory Towers

As the old girls had already discovered, Daisy was on duty in the dining-room at breakfast time, and they spoke freely in front of her.

'So, we are agreed,' said Sally. 'We are all going to the cinema tonight?'

'Yes,' said Darrell. 'The film starts at eight o'clock, so we should be back shortly before half past ten.'

'Are you wearing your famous diamonds, Mavis?' asked Daphne.

Mavis laughed. 'I think that they may be a little showy for a small cinema,' she said. 'I'd better leave them behind.'

'Well, for heaven's sake give them to Matron for safe-keeping,' said Gwen. 'It makes my blood run cold to think of them lying around in the drawer of your cabinet.'

'Oh, they have been perfectly fine there all week,' said Mavis, lightly. 'And they will be perfectly safe there tonight, as well.'

But the girls didn't go to the cinema that night. Instead they sat in the common-room, as quiet as mice, so that if Daisy happened to pass she would not know they were there. All except for Alicia, Darrell and Gwen, who were upstairs. Alicia lay hidden under her bed, which was opposite Mavis's, so that she had an excellent view if anyone came in. And jolly uncomfortable it was too! Darrell and Gwen, meanwhile, sat on a window seat in an alcove in the passage outside the dormitory, hidden from view by a heavy curtain.

The time seemed to pass very slowly indeed for all concerned, as there was nothing they could do to occupy themselves, not even talk! But, just as the three upstairs were beginning to wonder if Daisy was going to take the bait, they heard the sound of feet padding softly up the stairs. Gwen clutched at Darrell's arm, and Darrell patted her hand reassuringly, holding a warning finger up to her lips.

In the dormitory, Alicia tensed as she heard the door open, then blinked rapidly as the light was switched on. Hardly daring to breathe, she watched as a pair of legs, clad in black stockings and sensible black shoes, came into view and made straight for Mavis's bed. The intruder had her back to Alicia now, so the girl took a chance and stuck her head out so that she could get a good look. Yes, it was Daisy all right! And she was helping herself to Mavis's 'diamonds'!

Quickly, Alicia drew her head back in, then Daisy switched off the light and went out, closing the door behind her. Instantly, Alicia emerged from her hiding-place, yelling at the top of her voice, 'DARRELL!'

This was the signal that they had agreed on, to let Darrell and Gwen know that Daisy had taken the jewellery, and both girls jumped out from behind the curtain, confronting the startled Daisy.

The maid hardly knew what to think for a moment. That yell had come from the dormitory, but there had been no one in there a moment before. And what were two of the old girls doing up here when they were supposed to be at the cinema? Then Daisy heard a door open behind her, and saw Alicia coming out of the dormitory, a grim expression on her face and, all at once, she realised the trap she had fallen into.

'Let us see what you have in your pocket, Daisy,' demanded Darrell.

'W-why, nothing,' stammered Daisy, trying to bluff it out.

'Don't lie, Daisy,' said Alicia. 'You have Mavis's jewellery in there, for I saw you take it.'

'I – I was taking it to put in Matron's safe,' said the girl, sounding desperate now. 'You see, I overheard you talking at breakfast, and –'

'Don't lie!' said Gwen scornfully. 'You were stealing them, just as you stole the cufflinks I bought for my father.'

Daisy turned pale, and suddenly all the fight seemed to go out of her. Then she glared at Gwen and hissed, 'Yes, I took the jewellery. But I wasn't going to keep it for myself, oh no. I was going to plant it in your room, so that it looked as if *you* had taken it, then Miss Grayling would have had no choice but to dismiss you – the high-and-mighty Miss Lacey! But you're not so high-and-mighty now, are you?'

Gwen shrank back as though she had been slapped, quite sickened by the hatred in the maid's voice.

Seeing that Gwen looked as if she was about to faint, Alicia said to Daisy, 'Be quiet! You're coming along to Miss Grayling's study with us, right now.'

Daisy did not protest, for she knew that the game was up, and walked along sullenly with the three girls to the Head's room.

Fortunately, Miss Grayling had not yet gone to bed, and she called out, 'Come in!' when Darrell tapped on her door.

She raised her brows when the three girls, accompanied by a reluctant Daisy, entered, and asked, 'Is something the matter?'

'I'm afraid that there is,' said Darrell. 'We have just caught Daisy stealing Mavis's jewellery.'

There was no need for the Head to ask Daisy if this was true, for guilt was written all over the girl's face. Miss Grayling felt shocked and dismayed, for Daisy had been at the school for a number of years, and although she was a little too fond of gossiping at times, the Head would have sworn that she was of good character. It saddened her deeply to find out that she had been mistaken.

'There is more, I am afraid, Miss Grayling,' said Gwen, and she went on to tell the astonished Head mistress the other things Daisy was suspected of doing.

Really, thought the Head, it seems quite unbelievable

that all this has been going on under my nose, and I didn't have the faintest idea!

'But Gwen, my dear, I don't understand,' she said. 'Why on earth didn't you report the loss of your cufflinks?'

'I – I didn't want to make a fuss,' said Gwen, looking down at the carpet. 'I thought that if I caused trouble, you might not want to keep me on here.'

'I see,' said Miss Grayling quietly. Then her expression hardened as she turned to Daisy, and said, 'Please hand over the jewellery that you stole.'

Red-faced, Daisy put her hand into the big pocket of her apron, and pulled out Mavis's necklace and earrings, placing them on the Head's desk.

Miss Grayling glanced at them, then said, 'And you intended to plant these in Miss Lacey's room so that I would dismiss her. All because she treated you unpleasantly many years ago. What a low and spiteful act, Daisy.'

Both Daisy and Gwen turned red at this, for Gwen did not like to be reminded of how mean she had been to Daisy.

'And am I to understand that you also masqueraded as Miss Lacey, and locked poor Lizzie Mannering in the shed?' asked the Head.

'Yes,' admitted Daisy. 'I knew that the first formers were having a feast, you see, for they had asked me to provide them with lemonade. And I knew that Miss Lizzie would be snooping around, for I overheard them discussing how to get the better of her. I already had Miss Lacey's clothes, for I had washed them for her, and I had taken the hat from her room when I stole the cufflinks. All I had to do was borrow a wig from the costume box behind the stage that is used for plays and concerts.'

'You seem to have done quite a bit of snooping around yourself,' said the outspoken Alicia in a hard voice. 'You were outside our common-room the other night, weren't you, and heard us talking about visiting Gwen's class-room the following morning. So you were able to sneak in first and write that horrible message on the blackboard.'

Daisy hung her head but said nothing and, at last, Miss Grayling said, 'Daisy, you will pack your bags tonight and leave Malory Towers tomorrow morning. But first, I must insist that you give Miss Lacey her cufflinks back.'

So the three old girls, Daisy and Miss Grayling went along to the maid's room, up in the attics. There, Daisy produced a rather battered suitcase from under her bed, and threw open the lid to reveal a small jewellery box containing the cufflinks, Gwen's hat, a blonde wig and a bottle of very expensive perfume.

'Is this yours, Gwen?' asked Darrell, holding up the bottle.

'No,' said Gwen, puzzled. 'I have never seen it before.'

'I took it from Miss Amy,' said Daisy. 'Oh, I didn't steal it from her, but what I did was just as bad. I made her give it to me in return for keeping quiet about something. I shan't tell you what.'

'Well, I'm glad to see that you still have *some* decency,' said Alicia scornfully.

Suddenly, Daisy's legs began to tremble, and she sat down abruptly on her bed, looking up at Miss Grayling, and saying in little more than a whisper, 'Will you have to call the police?'

The Head looked at Gwen, and said, 'That is for Miss Lacey to decide, as she has borne the brunt of your spite.'

'I don't want the police involved,' said Gwen at once. 'Daisy, you have behaved very badly indeed, but I am partly to blame because of the shameful way I treated you all those years ago. I think that losing your job and being sent away from Malory Towers is punishment enough.'

'A just decision, I think,' said Miss Grayling. 'Daisy, you will remain here until morning. I shall inform the housekeeper that you are leaving in the morning because of some family crisis. Any wages that you are owed will be sent to your home.'

'Thank you, Miss Grayling,' said Daisy, feeling quite light-headed with relief that the police weren't going to be called. Then she looked at Gwen, and said, 'Thank you as well. I'm sorry, but it should comfort you to know that I have hurt myself far more than I have hurt you.'

'It doesn't,' said Gwen quietly. Then, followed by Miss Grayling and the others, she turned and left the room.

'Phew! Thank goodness that's over!' said Darrell,

when they were all out on the landing.

'Well, I am thanking goodness that I allowed you girls to hold your reunion here,' said Miss Grayling. 'But for you, we might never have got to the bottom of this, and Daisy could have continued persecuting Gwen next term.'

'Next term?' said Gwen, hardly able to believe her ears. 'Miss Grayling, do you mean . . .'

'Yes, Gwen,' said Miss Grayling with a smile. 'I would like you to return to Malory Towers in September and teach the girls who will be moving up into the sixth form.'

'Marvellous news, Gwen!' cried Darrell, patting the girl on the back.

'Simply super!' said Alicia. 'Come on, girls, let's go back to the common-room and tell the others everything that had happened.'

'Oh, I've still got Amy's perfume,' said Darrell, suddenly realising that she was clutching the bottle.

'Well, you can give it to her tomorrow,' said Alicia, grabbing Darrell's arm and pulling her towards the stairs. 'Come *on*! The others must be on tenterhooks!'

Miss Peters and the third formers arrived back at school on Friday morning, the last day of term. Fortunately, the third formers had packed their trunks before leaving for their camping trip, so they had nothing to do but wait for their parents to arrive.

For everyone else, though, it was a bustle of last-minute activity as trunks and night cases were packed.

'This quite takes me back,' said Irene, haphazardly stuffing things into her night case. 'I can almost imagine that I am a first former, going home for the holidays.'

'Yes, you tried to steal my pyjamas then!' said Alicia, snatching them back from Irene.

'Thank goodness we only have night cases to fill this time, and not trunks!' said Daphne. 'How I do hate packing!'

In the sixth-form dormitory, meanwhile, Felicity went up to Amy and said, 'I almost forgot! Darrell came up to me after breakfast, and asked me to give you this.'

'My perfume!' cried Amy, absolutely delighted to have it back again.

'Yes, it was found in Daisy's room,' said Felicity, and Amy flushed a little as she remembered giving it to the maid in return for her silence.

The news of Daisy's disgrace had flown round the school, of course, but with the excitement of the last day of term, no one had said very much about it.

At last, the sixth formers were packed, and they carried their night cases down to the big hall, all of them feeling rather solemn suddenly.

The old girls were already there, and Darrell smiled at Felicity as she saw her coming down the stairs.

'How do you feel?' she asked when Felicity came up to her.

'Excited, sad – all mixed up, really!' laughed Felicity.

'Just the way I felt on my last day,' said Darrell.

All the mistresses, as well as Matron, had gathered in

the big hall, for everyone wanted to say goodbye to the old girls, as well as to the departing sixth formers.

Mam'zelle Dupont grew quite tearful as she hugged everyone in turn, and Nora disgraced herself by bursting into tears too, though everyone assured her that it was quite understandable.

At last the big coaches that would take the train girls to the station arrived, and there were a great many emotional farewells.

The hall seemed a great deal bigger and emptier once they had left, and Felicity said to Darrell, 'I do hope that Mother and Daddy don't arrive too soon. I want to make my last moments at Malory Towers last as long as possible.'

'They may not be your very last moments,' said Sally, overhearing this. 'Who knows, you may want to arrange a reunion of your own in a few years.'

'Yes, that would be fun,' said Felicity, brightening a little. 'It makes me feel less sad to think that I might come back one day.'

Just then, Daffy came running up to Sally, grabbing at her sleeve. 'Mother and Daddy are here!' she cried. 'Do come on, Sally. Goodbye, Darrell! Goodbye, Felicity!'

'These youngsters just have no sense of occasion,' sighed Sally, shaking her head. 'I shall see you both in the holidays, I expect. Yes, Daffy, I'm coming!'

'Do you mind if we wait outside, Darrell?' asked Felicity. 'I think the sunshine might cheer me up a little, and I'd like a last look at the grounds.'

'Good idea,' said Darrell.

So the two sisters made their way outside to wait for their parents, each lost in her own thoughts as they looked at the gaily coloured flower-beds, and well-kept lawns.

Then, all too soon, Mr Rivers's car could be seen winding its way up the drive, and it was time to leave.

Felicity and Darrell climbed into the back seat and, as the car pulled away, both of them turned and looked back – and said a silent goodbye to Malory Towers.